Abington Community Library
1200 West Grove Street
Clarks Summit, Penna. 18411

1. Books may be kept two weeks and may be renewed once for the same period, except 7 day books and magazines.

2. A fine is charged for each day a book is not returned according to the above rule. No book will be issued to any person incurring such a fine until it has been paid.

3. All injuries to books beyond reasonable wear and all losses shall be made good to the satisfaction of the Librarian.

4. Each borrower is held responsible for all books charged on his card and for all fines accruing on the same

GAYLORD M

MURDER
BY THE
NUMBERS

· AN ELIOT NESS NOVEL ·

MURDER
BY THE
NUMBERS

MAX ALLAN COLLINS

ST. MARTIN'S PRESS • NEW YORK

Design by Judith A. Stagnitto

Library of Congress Cataloging-in-Publication Data

Collins, Max Allan.
    Murder by the numbers / Max Allan Collins.
       p.   cm.
    ''A Thomas Dunne book.''
    ISBN 0-312-08856-6
    I. Title.
    PS3553.C4753M8   1993
    813'.54—dc20   92-41157
                                                 CIP

First edition: March 1993

10 9 8 7 6 5 4 3 2 1

This novel is in memory of
Jack Lockridge
who made me love history
and, along the way, taught me how to think

This is a novel based upon events in the life of Eliot Ness. Although the historical incidents in this novel are portrayed more or less accurately (as much as the passage of time, and contradictory source material, will allow), fact, speculation and fiction are freely mixed here; historical personages exist side by side with composite characters and wholly fictional ones—all of whom act and speak at the author's whim.

The city lived and breathed and slept as usual. People were lying, stealing, cheating, murdering; people were praying, singing, laughing, loving and being loved; and people were being born and people were dying.

—CHESTER HIMES

MURDER
BY THE
NUMBERS

· PROLOGUE ·

MARCH 7, 1933

1

Toussaint Johnson, a big loose-limbed man in a baggy light brown suit, the dark brown band of a shoulder holster cutting under a blood-red tie across a cobalt-blue shirt, looked headless in the black night. That was how black he was. Under a misshapen charcoal fedora, his kinky hair was cut back to the scalp and his face had a harsh, angular, African look; his bark-brown eyes, under deceptively sleepy hoods, were as piercing as a well-placed gunshot.

Johnson, a detective working out of the so-called "Roaring" Third Precinct on Cleveland's east side, was ambling across 89th Street, having left his Chevy in the parking lot of the Antioch Baptist Church up the block. It was a pleasant, cool Monday night, approaching ten o'clock, and he was on his way to see Rufus Murphy, the numbers king.

Fifty-five years old, fat and sassy, Rufus Murphy lived in a well-tended three-story yellow wood-frame house on the east side of this residential street. The Negroes who lived around here, on the edge of the white working-class neighborhood known as Hough, were primarily professionals— doctors, lawyers, teachers—but then Murphy was a professional of sorts himself.

The numbers game—actually games, namely "policy" and "clearing house," known derisively in some quarters as "the nigger pool"—was big business in the black ghetto of Cleveland. Both policy and clearing house were illegal lottery games, the former based on a drawing of numbered balls from a rotating drum, the latter on the daily stock exchange numbers in the newspaper.

An army of collectors, known more commonly as runners, solicited players among the denizens of black Cleveland, middle class and poverty stricken alike, giving them slips with their chosen numbers, keeping duplicate slips. Working for ten percent of what they collected, and tips from winners, the runners turned in their slips and cash to a controller. Each controller had charge of fifty or so runners, and kept five percent of the day's haul before turning the balance over to an operator, or "king," like Rufus Murphy, who was one of the Big Four numbers kings in the city.

In black Cleveland, Murphy was anything but a criminal. Affable, approachable Murphy was a symbol of financial stability in the midst of the Depression. He owned taverns, restaurants, and a food market; he provided backing for other Negro entrepreneurs; he was a patron of local charities, setting up college scholarships for outstanding Negro students. Ministers, civic leaders, and politicians had reason to smile upon Rufus Murphy, whose pocketbook, after all, smiled on them. He—like the numbers game—was a community institution.

In a few short years, Toussaint Johnson had become an institution in the Roaring Third, himself. Johnson was one of the city's three black detectives—out of a dozen colored cops total—and was tougher than a nickel steak and honest as a mother's love. He carried a custom-made nickel-plated .38 with a six-inch barrel under either arm; it was said that a man once fainted at the sight of the shiny cannons. Thirty-four years old, Johnson was murder on purse snatchers, burglars, con men, and muggers; he was bloody murder on any whites working any racket on the black streets.

He crossed the long, gently sloping lawn, past the neatly trimmed shrubbery hugging Murphy's house and went to the side door near the freestanding two-car garage at the end of a paved drive. He knocked once, sharp and hard, like a rifle shot. He waited. He did not knock again.

Finally the door opened and Rufus Murphy, all five-foot-eight and two-hundred-fifty pounds of him, stood in the doorway. Murphy's freckled brown face was split in a wide smile in which several gold teeth winked; his head was round as a cantaloupe and just as bald. He was wearing a white apron over a dark green silk shirt, its sleeves rolled up to expose brown arms above catcher's-mitt hands on which several massive gold, diamond-set rings resided, including one bearing a garish Elks Lodge insignia; his pants were a shiny olive gabardine above square-toed yellow pigskin Florsheim bluchers.

Spreading his arms like a pudgy messiah, Murphy said, "Toussaint, my man, come in, come in. . . ."

He opened the door and Johnson lumbered in, taking off his hat.

"Smells mighty fine," the detective said, glancing around the large modern red-and-white kitchen. Several pots and pans were steaming on the stove, but the enamel-topped table, partly covered by a red-and-white checkered cloth, was already set for two with two covered serving dishes and an overflowing platter of cornbread.

"I sent Mamie to bed," Rufus said, referring to his wife of twenty-odd years, an ex-showgirl who was pleasantly plump now. He seemed proud of himself. "I cooked this mahse'f."

"I hear you was the best cook the Santa Fe Railroad ever had," Johnson conceded with a mild smile.

Rufus gestured for Johnson to sit down, which the detective did. The pudgy numbers boss uncovered the dishes and said, "He'p yourself, son," and Johnson filled his plate with well-seasoned boiled collard greens, okra, and pig's feet from the larger of the two dishes, and steaming black-eyed peas from the other, then speared a hunk of cornbread off the platter.

From the refrigerator Rufus got two sweating bottles of Pabst Blue Ribbon beer, opened them both, gave one to Johnson. Rufus immediately drained his beer, then popped himself open another.

The two men sat and ate and drank in silence for several minutes.

"Done yourself proud, Mr. Murphy."

"Rufus, son. After all these years, ain't we friends enough for first names?"

Johnson swallowed a slimy bite of okra, savoring it before saying, "This is business. Your hospitality is 'preciated. But first names ain't for business."

Rufus sighed. His muddy brown eyes were bloodshot. He wiped a piece of cornbread through his black-eyed peas and munched it almost absently, saying, with his mouth full, "So it's a business call, then?"

"You know why I asked to see you."

"It ain't payday, is it?"

"That unkind, Mr. Murphy. And uncalled for."

Rufus shook his head; he seemed sad. "You're right. Sure I know why you're here. But maybe I'm not a worryin' man like you is, Toussaint."

"I'm not worried, Mr. Murphy. It ain't *my* feet that's to the fire."

The features of Rufus's face clenched like a fist. "The great 'Two-Gun' Toussaint, afraid of some goddamn dago pissant bastards . . . it ain't like you."

Johnson didn't flinch at the insult. He said, "I ain't afraid. And I ain't worried. But you ought to be."

Last week, a quartet of white hoodlums, led by Little Angelo Scalise himself, broke up a Murphy-backed policy drawing, brandishing revolvers, confiscating the small drum-shaped container and its seventy-eight consecutively numbered balls, terrorizing the handful of hired help and the hundred or more patrons.

"Tell your fat boss," Little Angelo had said, "he can get his equipment back by seein' Black Sal."

Black Sal was white. Or dago white, anyway: Salvatore Lombardi, one of the big boys of the Mayfield Road mob, who

controlled bootlegging, gambling, and prostitution every-
where in Cleveland but the black ghetto.

"So fuckin' what?" Rufus said, talking through the fog of
the steaming dishes between them. "Little Angelo and his
tally goons been making ugly noises for months. Nothing
come of it. This ain't their side of town. They don't understand it."

"They don't got to understand nothin'. All they got to do
is get rid of you and hire some willin' niggers."

Rufus stood up and slammed his hand flat on the table; the
dishes rattled. "They ain't gettin' rid of me. I ain't goin'
nowhere!"

"When the big bell rings," Johnson said calmly, nibbling
at a piece of pig's foot, "all our black asses is up for grabs."

Rufus was trembling; whether with rage or fear, Johnson
couldn't tell. "What are you sayin'? They gon' try and kill old
Rufus?" His laugh was as harsh as it was unconvincing.
"Bunch of candy-ass paddies gon' come to my part of town
and play *that* game?"

"Why not? Mr. Murphy. Please. Sit down. Enjoy this fine
feast you made. I ain't the enemy."

Rufus swallowed, seeming embarrassed suddenly, and he
sighed and sat. "What are they doin' here, anyway? The
numbers ain't their game. It ain't never been a white man's
game."

"I don't know about that. My mama said the Spanish
conjured it."

"The Spanish ain't white."

A smile cracked Johnson's African mask of a face.
"Whiter than us, but so what? The wops are movin' in.
Prohibition is yesterday. Today it's a *new* racket they need."
Johnson chuckled. "Ever since the income-tax boys took
notice of your pal Holstein in Harlem, the world knows just
how high off the hog you policy kings is livin'."

A forgotten piece of cornbread in his hand, Rufus studied
his half-eaten plate of collard greens, okra, and pig's feet like
a gypsy lady trying to divine a winning number from her

crystal ball. Without looking up, he said, "They sent me a message."

Johnson looked up from his food, sharply. "What sort of message?"

Rufus got up, got himself another beer, opened it, drank half of it in one gulp, then sat again and winced as he said, "Frank Hogey sent one of his boys over to see me."

Hogey was the only white among black Cleveland's four policy kings. Most of his staff was colored.

With a weary shake of the head, his eyes glittering with anger, Rufus said, "Hogey's gonna go in with Lombardi. As a partner. I been offered the same deal."

"Which is what?"

"Black Sal gets twenty-five percent."

"For doin' what?"

"For doin' nothin'!" Rufus squeezed the piece of corn-bread in his hand and yellow fragments of it popped from his sudden fist like teeth. "Hunky bastards. Why should I?"

Johnson shrugged. "Make a counter offer, why don't you? Offer 'em ten percent."

"Why the fuck should I?"

"They got the power, man. They got City Hall sewed up tighter than Dick's hatband. They got all them white cops in their pocket and more tally torpedoes than Carter's got pills."

"What the hell am I payin' *you* for?"

Johnson looked at him coldly. "I give you what protection I can. I can't protect you against the will of God and I can't protect you against this."

Rufus was almost sputtering now. "What the hell does Councilman Raney have to say about it?"

"He says you better play along."

"Shit, man! They got Raney in their pocket, too? Shit."

This disparagement of Councilman Eustice Raney made Johnson bristle. Raney was Johnson's political godfather. The two men had both served in the 372nd Regiment in the Great War; every man in the 372nd was black, and every one had either been killed or wounded in the Argonne in September 1918. Raney, a successful lawyer who became the city's first Negro assistant police prosecutor in 1924, had been good to Johnson and other survivors of the 372nd.

"You know better than that," Johnson said, in sharp reply to Murphy questioning the councilman's loyalty. "But Raney's one of three black sailors sittin' in a stone white boat. They got some pull in the Republican party, 'cause of the colored vote, yes; but do you really think three colored councilmen can do doodley-squat when the Mayfield Road mob is in the game?"

Rufus rubbed his face with a cloth napkin, which he wadded up and discarded contemptuously; a tip of the napkin found its way into the pot of greens, okra, and pig's feet.

He pushed away from the table, stood, and said, "It's all talk. Them guineas ain't gonna find the Roarin' Third open to white folks. Let 'em try to muscle in. We'll send 'em all back to Murray Hill with their pale asses bloody and draggin'."

Johnson had finished his food. He took a final swig of the Pabst, which was still cold. The conversation, and the meal, had been brief.

The detective rose and said, "I wish I could help, Mr. Murphy. I truly do."

Rufus warmed to that and came around and put a hand on the taller man's shoulder; he squeezed. "You a good friend, Toussaint. I know you always do your best."

The cop's hard features went momentarily soft; he felt something tender for this fat little man who'd done so much for him and the community.

He said, "I'm givin' you good advice, Mr. Murphy. Accommodate these white boys. Render under Caesar that which is his and you'll stay a king yo'self."

Rufus sighed and smiled and shook his head sadly. "I stopped servin' white folks a long time ago, son, when I quit the Santa Fe."

"You still in the United States, though," Johnson reminded him, gently, as they stood near the door.

The fat policy king laughed softly and patted the younger man on the back. "What's your hurry? Mamie made some pecan pie yesterday; they's a couple slabs left."

"No thanks, Mr. Murphy."

"For Christsakes, will you call me Rufus! Business talk is over."

Johnson smiled; it was a surprisingly warm smile for such a hard- and cold-looking man. "Sure, Rufus. I'll see you next week. Payday."

Rufus smiled on one side of his face. "You never miss a one of those, do you, son? Here, I'll walk you out."

The night had gotten colder; the sky was as black as shutting your eyes. Johnson folded his arms and gathered himself in. But Rufus seemed to drink the chill in like another cold beer. They moved slowly down the gentle slope of Murphy's driveway, the small fat man gesturing as they walked and talked.

"White folks think the policy game is gambling," Rufus said, laughing softly. "But we knows better."

"We do?"

"It's a religion, son." Even in the dark Murphy's gold teeth gleamed. "It's mystery. It's lucky numbers. It's hot numbers. It's taking the numbers offa the license plates of a car that done rear-ended you. It's the number off your streetcar transfer that suddenly stares up at you and says *play me, I is the one*. It's asking a chile for a number . . . children are lucky, ya know, they're best ones to give you winnin' gigs." He stopped and laughed heartily, hands on his hips, as merry a king as Ole King Cole. Then he extended an arm and spread the fingers of one big hand, as if assaying his dominion. "It's a dream you have at night, it's the dream book that tells you what the dream means in the mornin', it's gypsy fortune tellers, it's the date the President died. . . ."

Johnson smiled a little, amused despite himself. "You love it, don't you, Rufus?"

"The numbers is a way of life," Rufus said, smiling, but

serious. "And it ain't got a blessed motherfuckin' thing to do with white men."

"Money," said Johnson, dispensing some folk wisdom of his own, "attracts whites like flies on shit. That is the surest bet in town, Rufus."

Rufus shook his head, but his smile didn't disappear. "You got no poetry in your soul, Toussaint. You got your papa's business head, but you ain't got a drop of your mama's poetry."

"Maybe so." Johnson put on his hat, tipped it. "Goodnight, Rufus."

"Good-night, son."

The policy king began to trudge up the gentle incline of his paved driveway, while Johnson paused for the easy flow of traffic to let him cross. He stepped onto the opposite sidewalk, glancing back with affection at the fat little policy king, who was approaching the bushes near his garage.

An explosion of flame burst from the bushes, like a bizarre blossom, and Murphy's left arm flew off his body and smacked against the side of the garage, the hand slapping the wood. Then the limb dropped to the cement like a log. Blood geysered and Murphy tottered, like a wind-up toy winding down, and turned questioningly, drunkenly toward the bushes, covering insufficiently with his right hand the bloody fountain spraying from his shattered left shoulder where his arm had been, and a dark shape rose from behind the shrubs and the second shotgun blast blew a hole in Rufus Murphy's chest and knocked him down, flat on his back.

Toussaint Johnson, the instant he'd seen the blossom of gunfire and heard the shotgun's roar, had crossed his hands before him and yanked the twin silver revolvers from his shoulder holsters. His usually impassive face became another face, one of bulging eyes and flaring nostrils and a huge hole of a mouth. Screaming in wordless rage, he bolted across the street and up the lawn and began firing, one gun at a time, like something out of a Western movie, blowing the night apart with his gunfire. Rufus was falling, but the assassin had already leaped from behind the bushes and was cutting through the space between the house and the garage into the backyard.

Johnson did not pause at Murphy's staring lifeless body, though it was jerking from reflex and spraying blood, speckling Johnson as he ran past, the detective nearly slipping in the already pooled blood. The assassin, thin as a blade, was knifing through the short backyard to the driveway of the adjacent house behind, where another vehicle waited, a black Ford sedan; both the assassin and the driver were white, that much Toussaint, even in the dark, on the run, could tell. Dressed in black, black fedora pulled down, the assassin carried the shotgun in his left hand like a relay racer's baton, and now twisted around to shoot a right-hand revolver at Toussaint, who hit the dirt, bullets flying overhead, crunching into the wood of the house behind. He went to return fire but the assassin was climbing into the rider's side of the sedan and the door shut just as Toussaint's next three thunderous shots puckered the metal door.

The car squealed away and was kicking up gravel as it made its turn toward the street by the time Toussaint was standing in the drive, ready to fire again.

He had missed the license plate, but earlier had caught a glimpse of the man's white face, a ghostly white male witch of a face with a pointed chin and a thin sharp nose; the pulled-down fedora obscured the rest.

Behind him he heard screaming.

A woman screaming. Mamie, Toussaint thought. Rufus's wife, wakened by the gunfire.

He ran back to Murphy, and indeed his dead friend was in the arms of his beautiful portly widow, her white nightgown a blotter of crimson from the still-flowing blood. Toussaint stood helpless in the drive, the two fabled silver revolvers loose in the hands of his dangling arms, pointing impotently, limply down.

The car was gone.

So was Rufus Murphy.

And Toussaint couldn't think of a damn thing to say or do to comfort Mamie. He fell to his knees; blood dampened his trousers; tears dampened his face.

He didn't say a word.

But in his head Toussaint Johnson vowed to God or the devil or anyone who was interested that the men who did this would pay and the color of their skin wouldn't mean shit.

Only the color of their blood.

· ONE ·

SEPTEMBER 26–OCTOBER 10, 1938

2

In the dimly lit, walnut-paneled lounge of the Hollenden Hotel, Eliot Ness was conducting a low-key, informal press conference with representatives of Cleveland's three major papers. It was Monday afternoon, just after three o'clock. Squeezed into one booth with Ness were burly Webb Seeley of the *News,* slim Clayton Fritchey of the *Press,* and lanky Sam Wild of the *Plain-Dealer.*

Ness was seated with his back to the wall, as was his habit, and wore a .38 revolver in a shoulder holster, which was not; a strange mixture of the diplomat and the adventurer, Ness only wore a gun when he felt it unavoidable.

He was director of public safety, the city official in charge of both the police and fire departments. Deep into his third year as the city's "top cop," Ness was still, at thirty-five, the youngest man in the nation to hold such a post.

Despite his age, Ness was a veteran of what the papers melodramatically termed his "personal war on crime." At twenty-six he had headed up the Prohibition Bureau's Chicago unit, a handful of Ness-picked men who with their baby-faced leader came to be known as the "Untouchables," thanks to a deserved reputation for withstanding bribes, threats, and political pressure. In his successful campaign to land Al Capone in jail, and in later efforts against the bootleg gangs of Kentucky, Tennessee, and Ohio, Eliot Ness earned a reputation for putting bad guys in the pen, while providing reporters with juicy headlines along the way.

In the last three years, in Cleveland, he had made his share of headlines for the men at this table, certainly, headlines that reached across the nation, due to the unceasing series of major criminal investigations this young executive had launched, made all the more newsworthy because that young executive often got out from behind his desk and into the fray.

First had come a no-holds-barred house-cleaning of the Cleveland P.D. that resulted in convictions and prison for six high-ranking crooked cops, followed by a wave of resignations from other panicking cops-on-the-take. Next the safety director had undertaken the search for the so-called "Mad Butcher of Kingsbury Run," burning out the Hoovervilles where the mass murderer lived and preyed. Most recently Ness had taken on crooked labor racketeers, and the result was again convictions and prison for the perpetrators.

The young safety director was beginning to show signs of the strain of all this; his boyish, faintly freckled face was looking fleshy and the placid gray eyes were pouched and bore crow's feet. His dark brown hair was touched lightly with gray at the temples, though a disobedient comma of dark brown hair touched his forehead in one stubborn flourish of youth.

Ness, dapper in a gray worsted suit with a knit shades-of-gray striped tie and monogrammed breast-pocket handkerchief, sat quietly with his hands folded; he might have been praying had his lips not worn a slight, playful smile. While the reporters drank their second round (bourbon for Wild, Scotch for Fritchey, and a beer for Seeley), Ness was working on his first drink: a cup of black coffee.

"You've never been known to pass up a drink, Eliot," Sam Wild said, with a good-natured edge. "Even when you *are* buying. . . ."

Wild was a pale, dark-blond scarecrow of man, his features angular, pointed, giving him a pleasantly satanic look; he wore a red bow tie and canary seersucker suit. Ness was accessible to all the press and counted many reporters, including those seated here, as friends; but Wild, assigned by the *Plain-Dealer* to cover Ness full time, was part of the safety director's inner circle, and sometimes unofficially took on investigative work for Ness that an official staff member dared not. And was as close a friend as this shy, private public official had.

Wild had, in the latter capacity, accompanied an inebriated Ness home from time to time; the irony of the world's most famous prohibition agent being a hard drinker was not lost on the reporter.

"Something's up, Eliot," Wild said. "Or you wouldn't be teetotaling it this afternoon."

"Something is up," Ness admitted, with an ornery child's smile. "I guess you know that we've been zeroing in on the Mayfield Road bunch."

"With labor out of the way," Fritchey drawled, nodding, "and the police department pretty well sanitized, it would seem about time you took those boys on, directly."

Webb Seeley shrugged. "You already chased Horvitz and Rothkopf and McGinty and their gambling interests out of the county."

"Hell," said Fritchey, "out of *state*—they're operating in northern Kentucky, now."

"Those boys," Wild put in, with one arched eyebrow, "are getting more and more into legitimate concerns. Even Chuck Polizzi is playing it cool. He's leaving it all to Lombardi and Scalise."

Ness was nodding. His smile had disappeared. He lifted a forefinger and waggled it like a scolding schoolteacher.

"Those two," he said, quietly ominous, "are next."

"Is that why you've been hitting the bookie joints so hard?" Seeley asked. "Getting so's a feller can't make an honest bet."

"What bookie joints are those?" Wild said, almost disgruntledly, swirling his bourbon in his glass. "Our esteemed safety director has shut down every bookie joint I know of. This city is getting as boring as its reputation, thanks to young Mr. Ness, here."

Seeley sipped his beer and said to Ness, "We lost count at eighty-four times in one month, when your men Powers and Allen kept raiding that same bookie joint . . . busted up the place so often the poor bastard bookie had to put two full-time carpenters on staff, to keep the place up and running. Finally said the hell with it and closed up shop."

"So what's left?" Fritchey asked. He laughed humorlessly. "The numbers game? You going to try to clean up the colored east side? That's rich."

Ness had an impassive expression, though a crease between his eyebrows belied that. He said, "First things first. There's another raid to make. Right here in downtown Cleveland."

"Another raid?" Seeley said. "What, is some penny-ante joint crouching in some corner somewhere? After you shuttered Maxie Diamond, what the hell is left?"

About a month before, Ness had invited the press along to view—and record—a lightning-swift raid on downtown Cleveland's biggest and busiest bookie joint, run by Maxie Diamond. A cigar counter and soft-drink machine provided the front for the East Ninth Street betting hall, and a bell and light system warned operators and players if any cops should arrive. Secret panels were built in the walls for racing sheets, telephones, betting slips, and playing cards to be stowed away, and in a secret room in the rear, a trapdoor and hidden panel permitted escape.

Diamond's success led to the construction of a second betting room in the basement; carpenters and electricians were put to work on what would have been a concrete anti-police fortress with steel doors. Ness had put an undercover man in the Diamond joint, and the undercover man tipped the safety director that the escape paths would be temporarily blocked because of the construction.

"We got some great pics on that little raiding party," Seeley said with a contented sigh. "Lucky for you Maxie didn't have those steel doors up. Even the great Ness couldn't kick in those babies."

There were smiles all around, Ness included, but Wild said, "Come on, fellas. Just because the bookie joints are pretty much shut down, that doesn't mean bettin' the horses in Cleveland is a thing of the past."

"Lombardi is taking a cue from his own racket," said Fritchey, casually. "Just like the numbers game—he's using runners."

"Right," Ness said, nodding. "Commission men. They work the streets, and call in the bets. Work for five percent of the bets plus a percentage of the winnings of their 'clients.' "

Wild raised an eyebrow. "Hell, that *is* a page right out of the numbers racket . . ."

"Black Sal Lombardi is nothing if not a shrewd business-man," Ness said, with grudging respect. "He's reduced his overhead and, at the same time, worked out a system that keeps crowds from congregating in one place and attracting police suspicion."

"With bookies continually calling in their bets," Wild said, "they don't have to haul around pocketsful of betting slips, meaning they won't get collared with any slips in their possession."

"No betting slips," Fritchey said, with a world-weary little shrug, "no evidence for a conviction."

"The perfect crime," Seeley said.

"No," said Ness, and a tiny smug smile tugged one corner of his mouth. "It's smooth, it's smart . . . but perfect it's not."

"Where's the loophole?" Wild said. "How do you raid a bookie joint that isn't there? What are you going to do, kick in the door of every phone booth in town?"

Ness sipped his coffee, savoring the strong brew, and the moment. He said, "Those phone calls the bookies make have somebody on the other end of 'em."

The reporters began to slowly nod.

"We've learned," Ness said, "that there is a 'nerve center,' with several dozen warm bodies working a battery of phones. That nerve center is within spitting distance, gentlemen."

"Yeah?" Wild said, sitting forward.

"It's on the seventh floor of the old Leader Building," Ness said, pointing. "Right across the street."

"Hot damn," Wild said. "When do we go?"

"Right now," Ness said. "You go call your photographers. Meet me across the street, in the Leader lobby, in five minutes."

The reporters were going even as the last word left Ness's lips.

Ness signed the check, slipped on his dark gray fedora, and, walking through the hotel's drugstore, stepped outside onto Sixth Street where a golden Indian summer afternoon awaited. He stood back from the stream of pedestrians for a moment and drank in the day. The Hollenden Hotel at his back, a fourteen-story red-brick Victorian structure on the southeast corner of Superior and Sixth, was the center of downtown Cleveland's social life. Public Square was a stone's throw away. City Hall, where the safety director's office was, was but a short walk north; there were several newspapers nearby, including the Plain-Dealer Building across the way diagonally. On the southwest side of Superior and Sixth was the tall gray nondescript Leader Building (the *Leader*, once a major Cleveland paper, had been swallowed up by the *News* years before).

This was the heart of the city—swarming with politicians, lawyers, newsmen, business executives, sportsmen. What better place for the nerve center of the city's gambling syndicate?

Jaywalking with care, the director of public safety crossed to the side entrance of the Leader Building, between a haberdashery and a cigar store. In the glorified hallway of a lobby, a bank of elevators on either side, Robert Chamberlin and several plainclothes cops were waiting.

"Got everything covered?" Ness asked his executive assistant. "Stairs, elevators, fire escape?"

"Yes indeed," Chamberlin said, a smile twitching under his tiny black mustache. "The press on the way?"

"They're scurrying after their photogs like rats after cheese."

"Knowing the sporting habits of the local press," Chamberlin smirked, "I can't think they'll be eager to see us close this shop down."

Chamberlin was a tall broad-shouldered man nearing forty, a lawyer who was equally at home with investigative and administrative duties. Shovel-jawed and sharp featured, with dark slicked-back hair, he had a military bearing that was partly offset by a wry sense of humor.

"Wild and the others do like to gamble," Ness admitted. "But they *love* a headline."

"Yes," said Chamberlin, "and we like to gamble, too, don't we? Tipping the press before a raid . . . they could leak it."

"That's why I waited till you'd had a chance to seal this building up," Ness said, "before I told 'em."

"There *is* a new wrinkle."

"Oh?"

"Shades of Maxie Diamond—they've installed a metal door."

"You're kidding; right in the hallway of an office building? That's a little conspicuous, isn't it?"

Chamberlin shook his head, no. "It's on the inside. I sent Al Curry up there posing as a confused Western Union messenger who went to the wrong office, and he got a good look. There's a receptionist in an outer office, and a big, heavy, gray steel door leads to the inner office, where the nerve center is."

Ness thought about that. "They'll be sitting at tables writing bets down on flash paper, with matches at their fingertips and wastebaskets at their feet. Damn."

"It's going to be tough to get in there before the evidence

is ashes," Chamberlin admitted. "The receptionist obviously is a lookout man—a better-looking lookout man than the Mayfield Road boys usually utilize, if Curry's to be believed . . . but a lookout man nonetheless."

"Nobody's up on the seventh floor yet?"

"Right. Garner and the raiding party are waiting on the sixth floor, as you instructed."

Ness checked his watch. He made a clicking sound and said, "The reporters will be here any second. You bring 'em up to the seventh floor at four o'clock sharp."

"That's just ten minutes from now. . . ."

"Right," Ness said, and took the freight elevator up to the sixth floor.

There he found Will Garner, vice cop Frank Moeller, and three more plainclothes cops waiting. Garner was a beefy six-four detective whose dark complexion and black hair reflected his Sioux heritage; he had been one of Ness's Untouchables in the Chicago days. Moeller was a pleasant, brown-haired, bullet-headed man who was about five pounds shy of heavy-set.

"Curry's covering the alley and the fire escape?" Ness asked.

Garner nodded.

"When do we go in?" Moeller asked.

"At four," Ness said.

"How?" the Indian said.

"You're going to walk right in through the receptionist's office; at four, somebody inside is going to unlock that steel door."

"Who's going to do that?" Moeller asked, wincing with confusion.

"Me," Ness said, lifting the metal lid off one of the two massive garbage cans that sat to one side of the freight elevator. The lid was like an ungainly, battered shield; Ness gripped it in his left hand.

The door to the fire escape was nearby; Ness walked to it, looked at Garner significantly, and said, "Four sharp."

Then Ness went out on the black metal stairway; the pleasant, nearly warm day seemed windier up here. He glanced down and waved to Albert Curry, who was standing guard below, by the loading dock. Then he climbed the fire-escape stairs to the seventh floor and moved along the catwalk of the 'scape till he came to the window he was looking for.

He knelt on the gridwork floor, one hand clutching the garbage can lid, fingertips of the other hand caressing the rough surface of the concrete building. He peeked carefully into the room. No drapes or blinds obscured the view; these crooks were bold. Or careless. He would have installed burglar-proof wire-mesh glass. But an operation like this had to keep moving, like a floating crap game, and renovations would seem too much bother, too much expense, for a temporary facility. Ness had counted on that.

At least thirty people were at work in the large office; several long, banquet-style tables filled the otherwise empty room, with people sitting on both sides, and everyone—except a few bouncer-like types who were either guards or supervisors or both—was busy on the phone every minute. And, as he'd figured, books of matches and wastebaskets were kept handy. He caught a glimpse of the formidable gray steel door.

He got out his revolver; the gun in one hand, the garbage can lid in the other, he continued to kneel, but didn't look inside anymore. He looked only at his watch, at the second hand as it glided around the face; waiting for four o'clock.

Four o'clock came and he stood. He took a breath, smiling, enjoying the adrenaline rush, enjoying this beautiful day, and he smashed the garbage-can lid into the window, shattering every pane in the lid's path, shards raining on the floor under the sill. Quickly but carefully, glass crunching under his feet, he hopped inside, tossing the garbage-can lid clatteringly to the floor, fanning the .38 before him, so it could take them all in.

"Everybody on your feet," he shouted, "hands in the air!"

Sixty eyes opened wide and thirty chins dropped to the

floor. The bookies, men of every size and shape but each one wearing shirts with sleeves rolled up, their coats on their chairs, slowly rose.

"This is a raid, gents," Ness said, moving along with his back to the wall; when he reached the steel door, he unbolted and swung it open. "No sudden moves . . ."

As if to contradict their boss, Garner, Moeller, Chamberlin, and half a dozen plainclothes men rushed in, and began gathering the evidence.

Soon flashbulbs were popping, and Sam Wild, lighting up a Lucky, smiled at Ness lazily and said, "You topped Maxie Diamond, after all—even bagged yourself a steel door."

Ness said nothing, but allowed himself a small, self-satisfied smile.

Wild erased it: "Now let's see how you fare on the colored side of town . . ."

3

Albert Curry, youngest plainclothes man on the department, was disappointed he'd missed the action. Keeping watch in the alley had proved to be dull and, while much of what any police detective did was perfunctory and routine, Curry had been spoiled. Being attached to the safety director's office meant consistently lively duty.

Curry was a fair-haired, pale, cherubic thirty and looked at least five years younger. He was standing beside his chief's black Ford sedan, leaning casually against the door, ready to drive him back to City Hall. He was watching with satisfaction and some envy as Bob Chamberlin, with the aid of several uniformed men, led a parade of disgusted-looking crooks in shirtsleeves and loosened ties out of the Leader Building into the back of a Black Maria waiting on Sixth; this was the second paddy wagon to be so filled.

Typical of his chief's style, this raid had gone off smoothly and quickly. It was barely four-thirty and thirty-one arrests had been made (thirty males and one female, the blond receptionist, who'd gotten a private ride over to the jail with a policewoman chaperone). Ness and Will Garner were upstairs combing the office.

From the alley Curry had seen Ness break the window and leap in that window, gun in hand. Well, maybe not *leap* (although the papers would surely put it that way); but Curry could hardly imagine another safety director in the country making such a reckless play.

Curry admired that, though his boss did get some criticism for being a glory-hound, for going out in the field and investigating and leaving the administrative duties largely to Chamberlin and others. His chief's reputation as "the G-man who got Capone" was an important publicity tool for Mayor Burton; Curry saw nothing wrong with that.

And to dismiss Ness as a publicity-seeking racketbuster was to ignore the facts: Ness was at the forefront of modern thinking in police science and criminology. A University of Chicago grad who studied with famed criminologist August Vollmer, Ness had modernized Cleveland's police department. He switched from cops walking beats to patrol cars with two-way radios, reorganized the traffic bureau, set up a juvenile delinquency unit, and much more.

Only once had Ness disappointed Curry. Last month, on the Mad Butcher investigation, Ness had captured the mass murderer but allowed the madman to be quietly committed to an asylum; the "butcher," it seemed, was the son of a prominent and wealthy friend of the mayor's. Though the safety director was the least political public official Curry had ever known, Ness had obviously caved in to pressure from Mayor Burton and the "financial angels" who had the slush fund that made possible, in this depression, many of the safety director's investigations.

Curry admired his chief no less for being human; in this hard world, in these hard times, it was hard to imagine a better man than Eliot Ness. But the young detective knew that the Untouchable was haunted by the compromise. Lately, Ness had thrown himself into his work even more obsessively than before. He looked bad, physically, to Curry; years older than just a few months ago. Ness worked late, then stayed out drinking with Wild and other news hounds, and must have been getting precious little sleep. Curry was worried for his boss.

The only saving grace, it seemed to Curry, was Ness's

girlfriend, Ev MacMillan, a fashion illustrator at Higbee's; she was apparently a calming influence, though she liked the nightlife, too.

Just as these thoughts were crossing his mind, Curry looked over to see Ness exiting the Leader Building with a wide grin and a spring in his step.

"I'll drive, Albert," he told Curry cheerfully, and went around to get behind the wheel of the sedan with the special EN-1 license plate.

Curry sat on the rider's side as Ness pulled out onto Superior.

"Are you through upstairs, already?" Curry asked.

"Garner's wrapping it up," Ness said, with a little shrug. Absently, he flicked on the police radio, keeping the volume at a low but decipherable hum. "We'll head over to Central Headquarters and question some of Lombardi's help, after they're booked. Maybe we'll get something."

"Wish I'd gone in with you."

"You didn't miss any action." He smiled over at Curry. "Things'll get lively as we close in on the Mayfield boys."

They waited at a stoplight.

Curry frankly wasn't convinced that the Lombardi investigation was going to flourish, now that the next logical step was to tackle the numbers game on the east side. That was foreign territory.

The light changed and Ness turned right, onto Superior.

"This little raid may turn out to be important," Ness said. "Oh?"

"The receptionist had three bank books in her purse, but they weren't *her* bank books. They were in the name of the 'Chestnut Magazine Subscription Service,' only I doubt they've sold any subscriptions."

"To a racing form maybe," Curry said, with a grin.

Ness grinned back; he had one hand on the wheel, very relaxed in the aftermath of his success. "Those bank books show deposits of three quarters of a million bucks."

Curry whistled low.

"If we can do a little backtrack bookwork, we're going to make it hot for Lombardi and company. I'll call my federal friends over at the I.R.S."

"If we can't nail 'em on the numbers racket," Curry said, nodding, "income tax evasion'll do just fine."

"It worked for Capone," Ness said, softly. He turned onto Payne. "What makes you think we won't nail them on the numbers racket?"

"Well, I . . ."

Ness laughed shortly. "You have a point. Working the east side is a riddle I haven't solved. Albert, I want you to look over the records of every Negro cop on the force."

"That won't be hard," Curry said, smirking humorlessly. "There are only ten of 'em."

"I know. That's a problem. How can we launch an effective investigation in the colored community when we don't have enough colored cops to do the job?"

"You don't need an army of men if you run an undercover operation. We've proven that time and again."

Ness shook his head no. "Every one of those ten cops is well known in that part of town. None of them could go undercover effectively."

"How welcome would Garner be, in Bloody Scovill? What's the Negro attitude toward an Indian?"

Ness shrugged. "I don't know. I'm not very knowledgeable about race relations, I admit. And this is a good argument for getting more Negro cops on the force. . . ."

As he trailed off, he was glancing at the two-way radio under the dash. Something had caught his ear. Curry hadn't been paying any attention to the broadcasts; apparently Ness had.

"What is it?" Curry said, sitting forward.

Ness shushed him and turned up the volume.

". . . Terminal, request back-up. We have a near riot situation here. . . ."

Ness plucked the microphone off the radio unit.

"This is Director Ness," he said. "What's the situation?"

"This is Patrol Sergeant John Wilson, Director Ness." The voice over the small radio speaker was tinny but distinct. "We have what is developing into a riot situation here at the east side market."

"Explain."

"We've got picketers blocking the doors and things are getting out of hand. They've been here all day but the crowd that's supporting them, well, their numbers have been increasing throughout the afternoon."

"Who are these picketers, the Future Outlook League?"

"Yes—Hollis and his bunch."

"How many men do you have?"

"There's a dozen of us."

"I'm on my way."

"But, sir—we need more back-up!"

"And I'm going to give it to you. Don't let this escalate into a riot, officer."

"I . . . I'll try, sir."

Ness clicked off, put the mike back on the radio unit.

He arched an eyebrow. "I guess we're going to get our feet wet on the east side, Detective Curry."

"What's going on?"

"You're familiar with the Future Outlook League, aren't you?"

"Frankly, no."

Ness turned right on East 17th, working his way over to Woodland and 40th, where the east market was.

"They've been around a couple of years. A Negro protest group. They're trying to get jobs for their people."

Curry snorted a laugh. "Well, hell. You don't have to be colored to be out of work these days."

Ness looked sharply at Curry. "No, you don't get it. They want jobs in their own neighborhood, in the east side stores whose clientele is colored, but whose clerks are invariably white."

"Oh."

"The Reverend James A. Hollis founded the group and

he's its president. They use pickets and boycotts to pursue their goals. They're peaceful but persistent.''

"How active is this group?''

"Very.''

Curry frowned. "Why the hell haven't I heard of them?''

"Do you read the *Call and Post*?''

That was Cleveland's primary black newspaper.

"Well, no, of course not.''

"That's the only place you're likely to read about the F.O.L. The white papers and the radio stations pay them no heed.''

Curry didn't know what to say about that, or what to think about it, either. He didn't consider himself prejudiced; nor did he consider his city to be backward in race relations. This was the progressive north, after all, not some redneck southern bastion of bigotry. But once the investigation into the policy racket began to rear its head, Curry had started to realize just how separate the worlds of the Negro and the white races were.

Curry glanced at the speedometer. The needle was nearing thirty-five.

"Maybe we should hit the siren,'' he suggested.

"No,'' Ness said curtly. "I don't want to add to the hysteria.''

Curry shrugged.

Ness looked quickly at Curry. "We don't need a repeat of what happened at Republic Steel.''

"You cooled that off well enough.''

"Eventually. But a lot of heads got cracked, first. I won't have my police beating up civilians. These things can turn into shooting wars in an instant. Do the words Memorial Day Massacre ring a bell?''

Ness was referring, Curry knew, to an incident in Chicago the year before when a parade of strikers was fired upon by cops; ten strikers were killed, hundreds were injured in the tear-gas-flung, nightstick-happy, bullet-ridden assault. It had happened in a field not far from where Ness grew up.

The Northern Ohio Food terminal was a sprawling affair

covering thirty-some acres from East 37th to East 40th between Woodland and Orange, with five massive concrete
buildings and an only slightly smaller auction hall. It was a
vivid, bustling world of fresh fruits and vegetables, wholesale
meats, live and dressed poultry, butter, cheese, and milk,
carted in from surrounding states and local producers as well.
The facility was less than ten years old, a modern, clean,
proficient wholesale market, serving the grocery, hotel, and
restaurant trades.

But it also served, with its four and a half acre grower's
market, the predominantly black residents of the east side.

"The Negro community that borders the terminal," Ness
said, "supports the market here to the tune of twenty grand
a day."

The two men were carefully crossing busy East 40th Street,
leaving the Ford parked across the way.

"Brother," Curry said, trying to grasp just how much
money twenty thousand dollars was. "No wonder they think
this joint owes 'em a few jobs."

"No wonder," Ness said dryly.

At the front entrance of the market building, a yellow-brick
structure a block long and half again as wide, a mostly colored crowd had gathered. Men, women, young, old, they
were restless and packed and noisy; Curry couldn't understand much of what was being said, but the mood of the
crowd seemed not one of anger, but curiosity: They were
pushing and shoving to see better. Ness pushed through them
like a knife through soft butter, saying "Excuse me" in a loud
voice with the edge of authority. Curry followed along, feeling some trepidation that Ness, apparently, did not.

The crowd was louder toward the front, and obviously
angry. A line of picketers with signs—NEGRO EMPLOYMENT
NOW; BOYCOTT WOODLAND MARKET; NEIGHBORHOOD JOBS—was
blocking the doors. They were well dressed, Curry noted;
suits and ties on the men, Sunday dresses and hats on the
women. They looked like a church group. Maybe they were:
One older man wore a clerical collar.

"Keep back!" a uniformed cop was saying; he had his nightstick in hand. He was speaking not to the picketers, but to the crowd, which was pressing in closer. Even the picketers seemed unsettled by the burgeoning mass of humanity.

Between the picketers and the crowd were ten cops, all white, spread out as thin as a pensioner's paycheck; they looked tired and exasperated and, Curry thought, frightened, though to the untrained eye the cops wore fierce expressions.

Ness looked over his shoulder at Curry. "They can't be doing any business in there," Ness said loudly, right in Curry's ear. "I'm going inside. Stay here!"

Ness moved forward; he spoke briefly to a cop, who recognized him, and several of the cops saw Ness and grinned, as if the cavalry had arrived. Perhaps, Curry thought, it had.

Ness approached the picketers. He sought out the older, dignified man, a preacher if his collar was to be believed, a tall, balding, bespectacled individual in the middle of the sign-carrying group. Ness offered his hand and the man, after a heartbeat, shook it. Ness spoke briefly, politely. The cleric nodded and allowed Ness to pass by him and enter the building.

Five minutes went by. Curry stayed on the edge of the crowd; without a uniform, joining the spread-out cordon of cops would be futile. He stayed there, alone in the crowd, one white blank face in a sea of black hostile ones, feeling for the first time what it was to be in the minority.

Part of the feeling was fear; but it was a more complicated feeling than that. He would lie awake that night thinking about it, as unsettled as the cops holding back this throng.

Over to his left, Curry saw an angry black woman in her fifties shouting at a cop, a florid-faced veteran who obviously knew his way around a nightstick. The cop moved close to the woman, and with his hand on the butt of his holstered gun, the nightstick tight in his other hand, began to shout back at her. His face was as red as the stripes on Old Glory, and the woman was matching his anger, the veins and cords standing out in her neck as though straining to keep her head attached to her body. Several other women, all of them, like their shouting friend, wearing floral dresses and Sunday hats, began screaming angrily at the cop.

Who suddenly drew back his nightstick, grabbing on to the woman with his other hand, clutching her arm.

Curry moved forward, but someone else moved faster.

Curry hadn't seen Ness come back out from the market, but he obviously had; he gripped the wrist of the nightstick-wielding hand of the cop, and pushed him back, firmly, but with no apparent anger. The cop, his grasp on the woman's arm broken, glared briefly at Ness, then recognized him, and the red drained from his face and he was as white as a lamb, and as sheepish.

The woman, whose anger had been replaced by fear, looked at Ness and smiled and nodded, and she seemed embarrassed, as well, but the crowd was still yelling, and closing in.

Ness moved back to the picket line and yelled, "Please!" at the top of his voice.

The crowd ignored him.

He yelled it again.

And again.

And the noise subsided just enough for him to get it out: "The market is closed!"

The noise picked back up, as that news was discussed, and then as Ness repeated, "The market is closed!" it again subsided.

"The market is closing its doors for the day," Ness said, loudly but not yelling. "Please disperse!"

It took several more tries. "You've closed the place down! Disperse peacefully!"

Finally, Curry moved toward Ness, as the crowd behind them began milling out and away.

Ness had approached the older, dignified man in the clerical collar and was speaking to him.

"The market manager agreed to shut down early," Ness was saying, "to put an end to this confrontation."

Normally the market stayed open well into the evening.

The preacher was nodding. "A wise decision," he said.

"Well, frankly," Ness said with a small smile, "they haven't done a hell of a lot of business today, thanks to you folks. You effectively shut them down, anyway."

"We did not resort to violence, Mr. Ness."

"I know that. If you had, you'd be in jail, Reverend Hollis."

So, Curry thought, this was Hollis, the Future Outlook League's founder and leader.

"And," Ness said, "the president of the stall operators association will meet with you tomorrow morning, here at the market, to talk about jobs for Negroes—if you'll agree to call off your picketers."

Hollis raised a forefinger. "I'll only do that if . . ."

"Mr. Hollis, I'm not a negotiator or a mediator between you and the stall operators. I'm just a messenger. There's a gentleman waiting inside to speak to you. I suggest you go inside, before the doors are locked."

Hollis nodded. "Thank you, Mr. Ness."

He offered his hand and Ness, twitching a smile, took it, shook it.

Hollis entered the market; his fellow protesters, their signs leaned against the side of the building, were relaxing, smiling, patting each other on the backs.

Ness approached one of the cops; they were watching warily as the crowd continued to disperse.

"Sergeant Wilson," Ness said, "gather your men, just over there." He pointed off to one side of the building, away from the picketers.

"Yes, sir."

Within five minutes the dozen officers were grouped in two rows of six, standing at attention.

"Relax, men," Ness said, with a wave. "You had a tough situation here today. I know you did your best. But some of you didn't help it any, bullying that crowd of onlookers." He looked sharply at the cop who had come within a whisper of using a nightstick on the colored woman. "What's your name, officer?"

"Peterson," the cop said, a defensive tone in his voice.

"What exactly did you think you were doing?"

"Well . . . my job. Keeping the niggers in line; they were disrupting the marketplace, sir."

Ness winced at the word "niggers." He walked over to Peterson and stood very close to him; looked him right in the face. The two men couldn't have been more than an inch apart, Curry figured.

"I don't give a damn what color they are," Ness said. "They're citizens who we're hired to protect and serve."

Ness backed away; he looked at all the men, hard. The sound of produce trucks could be heard in the background, grinding sounds that went well with Ness's barely controlled outrage.

"My men aren't going to go around beating up women with nightsticks." He glared at Peterson. "Is that understood, officer?"

Peterson swallowed. "Yes, sir."

Ness looked at every face. "Is there any man here who disagrees with me? Is there any man here who thinks it's our job to beat up civilians, colored or white?"

The cops, shamefacedly, shook their heads no, eyes avoiding Ness.

Without another word, Ness turned his back on them and with a nod to Curry walked away from the market.

"You drive," Ness said, as they reached the Ford.

Curry drove.

Ness was brooding.

On the ride to the Central Jail, Ness said only, "We do have our work cut out for us on the east side."

Curry couldn't have agreed more.

4

The following morning at City Hall, Ness gathered his key people for a council of war.

The men were grouped around one of three big conference tables that took up much of the floor space of the spare, masculine, wood-panel-and-glass office.

On one side of the table was Bob Chamberlin, looking almost professorial in a three-piece suit, smoking a pipe whose tobacco had a sickly sweet signature. Next to him was bullet-headed Sergeant Moeller of the vice squad, in a lived-in–looking uniform, cap on the table before him like a blue and white meal; he was an unpretentious, street-smart cop Ness had come to respect.

Detective Curry sat across from them, wearing a blue suit with a darker blue tie hanging loose; Albert looked bushed—the boy must have been up all night working, if the bags under his eyes were admissible evidence.

And next to Curry, in shirtsleeves but with his tie snugged tight, was big Will Garner, Ness's old comrade from the Chicago bootleg-busting days. The Indian was smoking a cigar of a cheap, harsh variety, its fumes battling the sweeter ones of Chamberlin's pipe.

Ness was at the head of the table, standing; like Chamberlin, he wore a three-piece suit and a tie. He rarely took off his jacket or loosened his tie, and today was no exception, though it was stuffy in the office. Too cold outside to open a window, not cold enough for steam heat to kick in. Pipe and cigar smoke swirled like fog.

"I've spoken to Prosecutor Cullitan," Ness said, tossing a fat manila file folder on the table before him, "and he's in back of us all the way. He's eager to take another of our 'epic investigations,' as he puts it, to the grand jury."

"Well then, Eliot, it's going to have to be the numbers racket," Chamberlin said, gesturing with his pipe. "We've done a hell of a job, harassing the bookie joints damn near out of business . . . but we don't have anything directly on Lombardi and Scalise."

"They're too well insulated," Moeller said, with a matter-of-fact shrug. "And not all the bookie joints are Lombardi's, anyway."

Ness nodded. "We tend to think of Lombardi as the 'Little Caesar' of the Mayfield Road gang, and he's certainly its single most powerful figure. But under the general umbrella of the Mayfield mob are half a dozen interrelated, overlapping but independent racket bosses."

"The numbers racket, though," Moeller said, lifting a forefinger, "is Lombardi's alone. Him and his cousin Scalise."

The haggard-looking Curry sighed. "But isn't Lombardi just as well 'insulated' where numbers are concerned, as he is in his bookie-joint interests?"

"Oh yes," Moeller said, nodding. "I know of eighteen direct underlings, and some fifty pickup men . . . Lombardi and Scalise own the colored east side, but you rarely if ever see them there, these days."

"*These days,*" Ness said, and pointed his finger at Moeller. "That's the key."

"What do you mean, Eliot?" Chamberlin asked, relighting his pipe.

Ness held up five fingers. "When Lombardi and Scalise muscled in on the policy racket, just five years ago, they came on strong—Young Turks, second-generation mafia intent on proving themselves. Meaning they did much of the work themselves . . . Scalise particularly."

Moeller was nodding again. "And Scalise does, on occasion, show up himself to this day, if some heavy intimidating needs doing. Besides which, that sadistic little bastard *likes* that sort of thing."

Ness flipped open the manila folder before him. Mug-shot photos of Lombardi and Scalise, enlarged to 8"-by-10" size, stared at the men.

"Unlikely as it seems," Ness said, "Salvatore Lombardi is only twenty-eight years old, and his cousin Angelo a year younger."

He pointed at Lombardi's picture; the face was a fleshy oval with a placid expression and baby-faced features, though the dark eyes were gun-metal hard.

"Sal took over the family bootlegging business when his papa, Anthony, 'Big Tony' they called him, was gunned down in 1927 by the Torellos."

"I take it Big Tony was a Mustache Pete," Garner said.

"Yes," Ness nodded, "a traditional Black Hand racketeer who considered himself a pillar of his immigrant community. In Chicago, of course, and New York, street toughs like Capone and Bugsy Siegel rose up and rubbed out the Mustache Petes. But in Cleveland, the Mustache Petes were never deposed, and today the Mayfield Road gang is run largely by their children."

Chamberlin knew all of this, at least vaguely; Moeller knew it by heart. But young Curry, and out-of-towner Garner, knew little and nothing, respectively, of the Mayfield Road gang's brutal history.

"Are these kids as tough as their daddies?" Garner asked, a nasty smile working around his stub of a cigar.

"Don't underestimate them, just because they didn't come up from the streets," Ness cautioned. "Remember two things when you're tempted to write off Black Sal Lombardi: His early years were spent in one of the roughest tenement sections of America; and at twenty-eight he's no younger than Capone was at the peak of his power."

Ness plucked the photo of Scalise out of the folder and slid it down the wooden table where the men could get a better look at the narrow-faced, hollow-eyed, liver-lipped gangster.

"As a case in point," he said, "Sal and his cousin Angelo, when they were both still teenagers, took care of the Torellos personally, in a series of killings that culminated in the slaughter at so-called 'Bloody Corner' back in '29."

"Were they convicted of those crimes?" Garner asked.

"No," Ness said.

Garner laughed silently, flicked his cigar ashes into a round glass tray, and said, "And today they got hired help, doing the dirty work."

"Providing the insulation," Curry added.

"Today they do," Ness said, and smiled nastily. *"Today.* Yesterday, five short years ago—no. Five short years ago they were Young Turks who wanted that side of town to know who was boss. Who to fear."

"They made their point," Moeller said, glumly, raising his hairy eyebrows. "Nobody on the east side, black or white, has ever offered evidence against them."

"Let's come back to that," Ness said. "Let's consider just what the nature of the Lombardi set-up is. Sergeant Moeller, for the benefit of the rest of us, who aren't as intimately acquainted the vice scene in Cleveland, share a little history with us. Please."

Ness sat down.

Moeller stood. "Five years ago, the numbers business in Cleveland was in relatively harmless hands. The 'Big Four' policy kings were Rufus Murphy, John C. Washington, Willie 'the Emperor' Rushing, and Frank Hogey. Hogey was the only white, but his help was mostly colored. Anyway, Lombardi and Scalise made threats, raided some places, finally began a shooting war. Murphy was killed, shot down in his driveway. Washington was shot, too, but not killed. Rushing and Hogey were worked over. Washington recovered, and retired, defeated. Rushing and Hogey are Lombardi's stooges, now."

"Before the Big Four were muscled in on," Garner asked, "did they control the whole numbers racket on the east side?"

Moeller shook his head, no. "There were any number of independent operators. These poor sons of bitches were made examples of by Lombardi. I can think of five, offhand, who were flat-out murdered, usually by cruising assassins."

"This wasn't all confined to '33," Ness said. "Over the years, whenever an independent operator has tried to find a niche on the east side, he's been rubbed out."

Back in '36, less than two months after he took the safety director job, Ness had encountered an example of Lombardi and company's discipline: A young independent policy writer named William Wiggens turned up dead in a ditch in the suburb of Pepper Pike. A colored youth barely twenty.

Moeller sat down, as Ness again rose, saying, "The late and unlamented Dutch Schultz of New York City, at the peak of his perverted power, never enjoyed a numbers set-up as profitable and perfect as Lombardi's. Schultz was smart enough, in the wake of Repeal, to horn in on the Harlem numbers racket . . . but he was content to take the bad with the good, the losing days with the winning ones. Here in the Forest City, though, there's no such thing as a losing day for the Mayfield gang."

"Why?" Garner asked.

Ness shrugged and smiled slyly. "They aren't gambling; they aren't risking nickel one. You see, they franchise individual operators, who take all the financial risk, while Lombardi and Scalise get a hefty forty percent of the take."

"Slick," Garner said, with a certain admiration.

"But keep in mind a single operator might lose as much as five thousand to ten thousand dollars in one day, if a certain number hits. And if any operator comes up short, on a losing day, he winds up in a ditch, courtesy of the Mayfield gang."

Ness dug in the manila folder and scattered several photos

of bullet-riddled corpses, one crumpled like a paper cup on a city street, another slumped bleeding over his steering wheel and, yes, several sprawled in ditches.

"Obviously, then," Ness continued, "Lombardi and Scalise have built up no loyalty whatsoever among their franchise holders. These operators, though tied to the Mayfield gang through what is essentially an extortion scheme, are in effect still independents. And they are the same people that Lombardi and Scalise terrorized into complying, some five years ago."

"So," Chamberlin said, nodding slowly, "that's why you keep emphasizing the past: You plan to get these operators to testify against Lombardi and Scalise, regarding the campaign of terror the two of 'em waged five years ago."

"That *is* the plan," Ness said. "That and a campaign of terror of our own—raiding numbers banks, policy drawings, disrupting the flow of business."

Moeller cleared his throat and Ness and the others looked at the uniformed officer, who shrugged and said, almost sheepishly, "No offense, Director Ness . . . but we don't have a very good handle on where the various numbers operations are located. First of all, they tend to shift around . . . . second of all, frankly, we're talking the colored east side here. And we have less than a dozen colored cops on the force."

Ness looked at Curry. "You've been going over the files on those Negro officers?"

"Yes," Curry said, blinking away tiredness. "Several of them have outstanding records . . . this fellow Toussaint Johnson, especially."

Moeller was shaking his head. "There's a problem inherent in using these colored cops. These boys do a good job, but remember that they got their positions out of patronage."

"You mean," Ness said, "through Councilman Raney."

"Yes," Moeller said, nodding. "And Raney, and I cast no aspersions, it's a part of that way of life over there, but Raney undoubtedly got his share of backing outa the Big Four policy kings, in the old days. They kept his campaign chest full."

Ness felt a twinge of irritation. "What's your point?"

"Well, again, I mean to cast no aspersions on the colored cops or their patron, but it's well known that these boys took the tribute of the policy kings. This Toussaint Johnson was said to be Rufus Murphy's bagman."

Ness looked at Moeller hard. "I don't like rumors, Sergeant Moeller. I like facts."

"I don't mean to share hearsay, Director Ness. But we have to be practical about this. And every cop knows that you got to pay attention to the grapevine."

"Well," Ness said, dismissively, "it's irrelevant. If my investigation into police corruption didn't turn anything up on these Negro cops, that's good enough for me."

"Fine," Moeller said, pleasantly. "But when it comes to the numbers racket, colored cops have their own vested interests, and their own way of seeing things. To them, the numbers ain't a crime. It's a way of life."

"We need an undercover man," Curry said, cutting in sharply, "and none of the Negro cops could be effectively used in that capacity, obviously. Too well known."

Ness looked at Garner. "Will, do you think you could fit that bill?"

Garner thought about it for a moment, puffing his cheap cigar. Then he shrugged and said, "I think I'd be accepted on the east side. I think I could take an apartment on Central Avenue. I could hang out. I could pick up on where policy drawings are being held. I could do that."

Ness smiled. "You do that very thing."

"But how," Curry said, with frustration, "are we going to get these policy operators to talk to us, much less testify against Lombardi and crew?"

"It's in their best interest," Ness said.

"They won't see it that way," Curry said.

Moeller said, "I think this young man is right."

"Then we'll educate them," Ness said. "We'll collar 'em on illegal lottery charges and offer them a free ride if they cooperate."

"It might work," Chamberlin said.

"It might," Moeller said.

Curry shrugged. "Worth a try . . . but it's not like you're holding a murder charge over their heads or anything. I think we need to find some other door to go in. This is Central Avenue, the Roaring Third Precinct, it's Bloody Scovill . . . it's their world, not ours."

Ness, feeling another twinge of irritation, said, "Do you have any suggestions, Albert?"

"No," he admitted, glumly. "But I don't agree with Officer Moeller about the unreliability of these Negro cops. I think at the very least you need to talk to them and get *their* suggestions. They know their part of town, and we don't."

The irritation fading, Ness said, with a gentle smile, "Albert, that's helpful. Thank you."

With a nod, Ness dismissed the men, stopping Garner momentarily to set up a time later that day to plan the Indian's undercover assignment in detail.

And he buttonholed Moeller for a moment, as well.

"This fellow Hogey," Ness said. "He's one of the original Big Four numbers kings, and he's white. Where do we stand with him?"

Moeller smiled on one side of his face and shook his head. "Hip-deep in nothing, is where we stand, Director Ness. He's the only holdover from the old days whose income hasn't dropped."

"Why's that?"

Moeller shrugged. "It's like you said—he's white. He's a glorified stooge, but he's in thick with Lombardi and Scalise. Color don't mean shit to Hogey, if you'll pardon my French."

"Sure it does," Ness said.

"Oh?"

"If it's the color green."

Moeller laughed shortly, nodded, and went out.

Ness went to the conference table, picked up the photos of Lombardi and Scalise, and pinned them to his bulletin board. Then he stood and studied the brutal faces in brooding silence.

5

That evening, a few minutes before ten o'clock, Sal Lombardi was sitting in a back booth of a bowling alley bar, drinking warm milk. The Pla-Mor Lanes, all forty of them, took up the entire second floor of a two-story row of businesses (florist, liquor store, fish market, druggist) on Kinsman Avenue, just into Shaker Heights. Sal owned the building, but the only business he owned there was the Pla-Mor. He didn't bowl himself, but his cousin Angelo did, and, besides, it was a good legit business. More than a front, or a money laundry: It paid its own way.

To look at him, you would think Salvatore Lombardi was the calmest man in Cleveland. A big man, five-eleven and two hundred and twenty pounds, neatly attired in a dark brown tailored suit with a green striped tie with emerald stickpin, he sat impassively with both hands caressing the glass of milk as if he were warming his hands. His eyebrows were as thick and dark as mustaches; his hair was dark and combed back, staying in place with a minimum of oil. Despite a hooked nose and hooded eyes that were as dark as his eyebrows, his olive-shaped, olive-complected face had a softness. His mouth was almost feminine, cupid-like, his small chin cushioned on a larger second one. For a thick-necked, thick-fingered gangster, Sal Lombardi had a surprisingly gentle demeanor.

Big Tony's "Fat Boy," he had been derisively called as a youth. A spoiled kid from Shaker Heights, a baby-faced mama's boy who in his teens had been forced to grow up, when his papa was murdered.

Now he was the most feared, most powerful man in the Mayfield Road gang. Or at least, he and his cousin Angelo Scalise together were the most feared; it had been a long time since Sal himself had pulled a trigger. Little Angelo, on the other hand, couldn't get enough of that.

Other than the milk, the only clue to an impartial observer that Black Sal Lombardi had a nervous stomach, a pre-ulcerous condition his doctor called it, was the almost imperceptible flinch of his face, a momentary wrinkling about the eyes, when somebody in a lane close to the thin-walled bar hit a strike. The echoing sound of bowling pins clattering against smooth wood made Sal jumpy. He didn't show it much. But it made him jumpy.

He liked nothing better than to hang out in a saloon with Ange or any of his other close Murray Hill pals, putting beers away, playing pinochle, bullshitting with the *paesans*. They'd talk broads, they'd talk boxing, they'd talk betting, they'd have a hell of time. Used to be a night in a bar was Sal's favorite way to relax.

Lately it had been different. He had never liked hanging out in the Pla-Mor bar, because the noise from the lanes was an annoyance. But lately no bar was pleasing to him, because booze, even beer, seemed hard on his stomach. The only thing that soothed his jittery belly was warm milk.

Even his goddamn food had to be mashed up for him or he couldn't stomach it; if he wasn't puking, he was constipated, and when he wasn't constipated, he had the fucking trots. If he'd had a sense of humor, he would have smiled at the irony of "Baby-Face Sal" (a nickname he had shaken years ago), now at the height of his power, reverting to a baby-like diet. But he didn't smile, or have a sense of humor.

It was that goddamn Ness. That goddamn fucking Ness. In the last six months that cocksucker had driven damn near all the gambling out of the county, and Sal had no piece of the northern Kentucky action—all of that was in the pocket of Horvitz and other Syndicate types too big to fuck with.

Fortunately, about the same time, Sal had sewed up local pinball distribution, and now—thanks to friends on the City Council—the machines were even legal. Many of Sal's enterprises were legal these days: real estate, linen supply, auto sales (he got his Cadillacs for cost, that way). Not long ago he'd made a small killing selling coal to the city of Cleveland.

No, the loss of income from the shuttered bookie operations was hardly crippling Sal, whose numbers action had grossed millions in the last five years. But it *was* annoying, and he had lost face.

Which was why Sal was here tonight, to meet with his cousin Angelo. More trouble, this time on the numbers front. Ness trouble. And, at the same time, out-of-town competitors trying to move in on them. Sal sighed, though it was barely noticeable.

He sipped his milk. He didn't mind the taste of it and had even come to love the soothing warm flow as it found its calming way to his twitchy belly. The glow of the warm milk hitting his stomach was better than Jack Daniel's.

Some people were going to have to die. No way around it. Sal regretted that, though not for any moral reason; he had a reputation for being shrewder, more far-sighted than his papa. Sal had displayed an ability to maintain reasonably peaceful relations with both his fellow racket bosses and the policy niggers in the Roaring Third. This earned him respect, which (although he wasn't conscious of the fact, exactly) he wanted more than money.

Though his earliest memories were of the same slum area where he now ruled (by proxy, mostly) the colored numbers racket, Salvatore Lombardi had grown up in the wealthy suburb of Shaker Heights. Big Tony, Sal's papa, was one of the first Italians to dare infiltrate that Protestant enclave, and Sal had spent most of his life living in the family mansion on Larchmere Boulevard; he lived there still, though Mama was gone now, and none of his brothers and sisters lived under that gabled roof.

Sal had warm memories of his papa, and much pride in the memory of the mighty immigrant Black Hand leader.

Big Tony Lombardi was only sixteen when he left a politically turbulent Italy behind, finding his way from New York to Cleveland, where he worked as a fruit and vegetable peddler. Getting active in the Black Hand, Big Tony used extortion money to buy his own wholesale sugar distribution company. He brought over first his three brothers, and then his boyhood chums, the Torellos, to help in the business.

Big Tony crowned himself corn-sugar king of Cleveland, making a fortune selling to bootleggers. He built a monopoly the good old-fashioned Black Hand way: He warned his competitors to quit and, if they didn't, had them shot.

Tears would warm Sal's cold dark eyes when he recalled the booming bass of his massive papa singing opera in the front parlor of the Larchmere mansion. And a startling sound it was, in that proper Protestant neighborhood. Not that any neighbor ever complained: Six feet tall, three hundred pounds, papa was a mustached bear of a man, a brute in diamond jewelry and silk shirts.

Sal remembered vividly when papa had pulled him out of the private Catholic school in Murray Hill, and sent him east to a boarding school. Sal had thought he was being punished for some unnamed something, not realizing a shooting war had broken out between Papa and the Torellos, and that it was dangerous for Sal, even with his bodyguard/chauffeur, to make that daily trek from Shaker Heights to Murray Hill.

So Sal, after fighting off an older kid who tried to cornhole him, ran away from the boarding school. He mugged an old man in a train station and took the train home. He figured his papa would beat him—though he'd only had a few half-hearted beatings from his father, when he was a lad—but when he peeked tentatively in the kitchen window, to see if Papa was home, his father looked up from his breakfast and saw his son, framed in the window. And papa began to cry.

Papa had gone to the window, reached his big arms out and hauled fifteen-year-old Sal up and in like he was a tyke, and hugged the boy fiercely and sat him down to breakfast. Mama had only smiled and served him. Sal's only other memory of that breakfast was glancing over at the window and seeing it filled with one of his father's ever-present bodyguards.

Sal wasn't entirely sheltered. He had some idea of what his father's business was. Papa had made sure of that, having teenage Sal from time to time accompany underlings of his father's, as they made their rounds, collecting money from bootleggers and loan sharks. Papa stressed early on the importance of business—that money was something you *made.*

"You will not inherit my money," Papa said many times, "you will inherit my business—and my good name. Take neither lightly."

Papa had taken him, when he was perhaps twelve, to see the corpse of a man who had betrayed him.

"This is what happens," Papa said, as they stood in a warehouse looking at a naked white corpse in pools of blackening blood, "to stupid people."

Stupid people, Sal was taught, were those who were too greedy, who were not loyal, who stole from their friends. It was made clear to the boy who was being groomed to be a "don" like his father that this could happen to him. It was also made clear that he could, and should, make it happen to those who betrayed him.

On an autumn evening in 1927, Big Tony and his brother Ralph, dressed in their usual natty attire, diamond stickpins winking in the neon night, entered the barber shop of Octavio Torello. A meet had been set up by Dominic Toscari, a confidant of both families, to settle the differences between the one-time friends, the Lombardis and the Torellos. The Torello barbershop had been agreed upon as a meeting place, because it was widely accepted that one does not shit where one eats. Therefore, violence was unlikely to break out.

Big Tony and Ralph were unarmed and had no bodyguards

with them. They would play some cards with their old friends, work their out their differences like gentlemen.

They walked to the rear of the shop, toward the card room, greeting acquaintances as they went, filling the air with friendly chatter. Then the two men entered the card room and the air filled with unfriendly chatter, from a crossfire of automatics.

Big Tony was dead when he hit the floor, seven bullets in him, two in the head. Uncle Ralph took a slug in the left leg and another in the stomach, but he was a younger man than papa, and he chased one of the gunmen through the barber shop, out onto Woodland Avenue.

"I got you now, you bastard," Uncle Ralph said, cornering the gunman in front of the butcher shop next door, charging him, and as he did, the gunman whapped Uncle Ralph in the forehead with the butt of the now-empty gun, driving it into his head like he was pounding a nail.

Uncle Ralph smiled, in a silly stunned way, and then fell on the pavement and died.

There were a number of witnesses, and the murder story in some detail was widely known in the Italian community. But no one talked to the police—not after the butcher, who got a good look at the killer who pistol-whipped Uncle Ralph, was shot in front of his shop, inches from where Uncle Ralph had fallen.

Cleveland had never seen a funeral like Papa's and Uncle Ralph's—silver caskets and brass bands and thousands of mourners lining Woodland Avenue, seven hundred autos winding their way to Calvary Cemetery. Big Tony Lombardi was beloved in his world, a man generous to a fault, free with his money and his favors to less fortunate Italian families on the east side.

It was important that Sal rise to his father's legend. To be a great man, a generous man.

And so, two years later, the eighteen-year-old Sal instructed his mama to drive him and cousin Angelo to East 110th Street, just south of Woodland, less than one hundred feet from the Torello barber shop where papa had died. Portly Mama, still in widow-black, her gray-touched black hair in a bun, her tiny kind eyes behind round black-framed glasses, called out to a man in the front of the barber shop. She was behind the wheel and the man had to lean in the passenger's side window. With a small, sweet smile she asked him to fetch Dominic Toscari at the nearby Torello sugar warehouse.

"Tell him Mrs. Lombardi wishes a word with him," she said.

Dominic—a swarthy, stocky, cocky fellow—obediently complied, swaggering up to the black Cadillac limo with a smile and a ready, "Hello, Mrs. Lombardi—what can I do for you on this fine day?"

"You can die, bastard," Sal said from the back seat, and he leaned out his window and began firing his revolver. Dominic's smile barely had time to leave his face as he twitched and danced and died.

Little Angelo jumped out of the car, on the street side, and came around and put a few bullets into the corpse, just so he wouldn't feel left out. Then, in a touch one of the papers referred to as "the melodramatic gangland calling card of death," Angelo dropped an ace of spades on the body of Big Tony's betrayer.

And the big car roared away, with Mama at the wheel.

The aftermath was long and hard on the family. Sal and Angelo fled to San Francisco and hid out. Mama was arrested on a first-degree murder charge. The prosecutor made it clear to Mama that she would be released if her son and nephew gave themselves up. The Lombardis, old Black Hand family that they were, understood this tactic; their fortune had been built on extortion, after all.

Mama was tried and acquitted of the murder charge, and in February of 1930, Sal and Angelo returned to Cleveland and gave themselves up. It seemed the state's star witness, another cousin of theirs, had decided to move to Italy; the climate was healthier there and, besides, their cousin had come into some unexpected money.

The Torellos had fallen like leaves in the coming months: Sam was gunned down in Frank Milano's Venetian Cafe on Mayfield Road. Vincent Torello went for a ride in the country, the one-way variety.

The five remaining Torellos gathered in January of 1932 at the corner of Woodland Avenue and East 110th.

"What the hell is this about?" Octavio Torello demanded of his brothers.

They looked at him curiously. The wind was blowing snow around from flurries of the day before.

"We got your message to meet you here," Pasquale Torello said, shrugging.

In moments the men realized they'd been summoned by phone messages that none of the others had sent.

"It's a fucking set-up," Octavio said. "Get the fuck outa here, you guys . . ."

But the black limo was already pulling up, the snout of a machine gun already pointing its about-to-scold finger at them. The Torellos had time to go for their guns, but not to draw them, before the fusillade ripped into them, shook the life from them, dropped them rudely to the pavement, corpses overlapping, blood of one running into the other.

Bloody Corner, they called it now. That corner where the Lombardi-Torello feud had begun and finally ended. It started as business—the Torellos wresting away Big Tony's corn-sugar empire—and ended in sheer revenge. The massacre at Bloody Corner came at a time when corn sugar and bootlegging were fading into the past.

And the policy and clearing-house racket was beckoning to the future.

Those early strong-arm years—the Torello war, the muscling-in on the Big Four policy kings, the executions of various independent policy operators—had earned respect for Black Sal Lombardi and his formidable second-in-command, Little Angelo Scalise. Their well-earned reputation for violence had allowed Sal to maintain a comparatively peaceful reign of power.

As for the niggers on the east side, there had been no bloody uprisings, or even strikes by policy writers (like Dutch Schultz ran into).

As for the police, Ness had been so tied up fighting crooked cops and labor racketeers since he got in office, the policy racket had been benignly neglected.

Only now, word was, the safety director had Black Sal's favorite, fattest source of income targeted for special attention. Seemed fucking up Sal's bookie operations wasn't enough to satisfy that goddamn Boy Scout.

And to top it all off, there was this Pittsburgh problem that Angelo wanted to talk about. Sal sighed, sipped his milk, and waited for his cousin. The sound of a strike in the lanes made Sal jump a little and then the sound of a yelp, a painful yelp at that, really unnerved him. So much so that it almost showed.

Angelo strutted into the small, sparsely populated bar, laughing; it was a sharp, hacking laugh. Angelo's thick lips were spread to reveal large white teeth; his dark eyes were glowing with amusement. Wearing a gray bowling shirt with *Angelo* sewn cursively over one pocket, he was a thin, monkey-like man who stood five-foot-five. He strode up to the booth and clapped his hands once and said, "That kills me."

"You got to stop doing that," Sal said.

"What?" Angelo said, innocently, his smile dropping away.

"Hitting the pin boy like that. I heard him yelp."

Angelo slid into the booth, laughing again, but softly. "That kills me. Little bastards should move faster. I ain't got all day."

Angelo waved to the bartender. There was no waitress and no booth service, but in Angelo's case, that didn't matter. The bartender brought him a beer.

"So what's the story?"

Angelo shrugged, sipping his beer, wiping off a foam mustache. "Ness is heating up. He's gonna try to make the niggers talk."

"It won't work."

"It sure as hell won't. I'm spreading the word that any black bastard who talks to the cops is a dead black bastard."

Sal shook his head wearily. "How many times I got to tell you? You got to treat 'em right. They're people too."

Angelo made a guttural noise deep in his throat. "They're fucking monkeys," the monkey man said.

Sal's cheek twitched with disapproval. "I'm not saying you don't get tough with 'em when they deserve it. But you got to treat niggers with respect like anybody else."

"Yeah, yeah. Well the niggers ain't the problem right now."

"What is? Pittsburgh?"

"Fucking Pittsburgh, yeah," Angelo said, nodding. He finished his beer, waved for another. He leaned forward and waggled a finger at Sal. "We're gettin' too soft. We got to show some fuckin' muscle again."

"What do you propose?"

"There's only about a dozen of these Pittsburgh punks in town at this time."

"Are they Syndicate guys?"

"Who the fuck cares? They bleed like anybody. They got themselves plopped down in the middle of the Roarin' Third, offering the suckers odds of 500 to 1."

The normal odds were 600 to 1.

Sal sipped his milk. "What makes them think we'll let 'em get away with undercutting us like that?"

"They think we got our hands full, with Ness on our butts."

"Do they. And what do you propose?"

"I propose to kick their Pittsburgh asses outa town. Personally."

Sal nodded, but he motioned gently with one hand. "We have people who can do that for us. And if we spread the word to the nigger policy writers that we're going to pay more than the Pittsburgh boys do, well . . ."

"Hey, fuck that! We'll spread the words that any jig that works for the Pittsburghers is a dead jig, capeesh?"

The bartender quickly deposited the second beer before the animated Angelo and departed.

The dark little man pointed at himself with a thumb. "And I'm gonna take care of this personal. This is a matter of respect. Of making sure they know and everybody else knows that just because we run a smooth racket, that don't make us soft."

Sal thought about that. "A matter of respect," he said softly.

"Yeah. That's exactly what it is."

"I like that," he said, and smiled. "Yeah. Go ahead, Ange. Take care of it yourself. Have yourself some fun for a change."

The sudden sound of a strike in the lane just beyond the thin wall didn't make Sal flinch a bit.

Angelo finished his beer, grinned wolfishly, and said, "Guess I'll go out and bowl a few lines."

"And cripple a few pin boys?"

Angelo laughed. "You're a good guy, Sal. You may got a weak stomach, but you still got both your balls."

The little man strutted out, whistling "Heigh Ho, Heigh Ho," and Sal finished his milk and left.

6

Ness sat studying the Lombardi and Scalise files at the scarred rolltop desk in his City Hall office, a desk that had been with him since his Chicago days. It was Monday afternoon, and the day had been filled with routine but necessary administrative duties. Now he could have some fun. He began going over the records of the Negro cops, as well, which he'd had Curry drop off.

Toussaint Johnson was indeed an interesting man; his folder was brimming with commendations. But Moeller was right about Johnson's connection to the numbers game: The Negro detective had been at the scene the night Rufus Murphy was shot and killed.

Shortly before four, the intercom buzzed and his secretary's voice said, "A visitor, sir."

"Does he have an appointment?" Ness said, absently, still studying the Johnson file, not remembering having anything scheduled.

"No, sir. It's a Reverend Hollis."

Ness looked up. "Send him in."

The Reverend James A. Hollis entered. The tall dignified leader of the Future Outlook League, dressed in clerical black, approached Ness, who stood and met the man midway. They exchanged reserved smiles and firm handshakes. Then Ness offered Hollis a seat at the nearest conference table.

"Reverend Hollis, I do have a engagement at four-thirty," Ness said, respectful but firm. "I'm afraid I only have a few minutes for you."

"I understand, Mr. Ness, and I appreciate your seeing me with no notice."

Hollis's speech was so well enunciated, it sounded almost British, though a vague vestige of the South lurked in the mellow, resonant baritone.

"What can I do for you, Reverend?"

"It's what I can do for you, Mr. Ness."

"Really."

A handsome smile formed slowly in the dark brown face; but the eyes behind the wire-rim glasses were cool. "I do want to commend you on your conduct last week, at the market. People could've been hurt. Thanks to you, they weren't."

"Reverend Hollis, you're lucky *you* weren't. These boycotts and picket demonstrations may result in violence. We both know that."

Hollis nodded. "Progress has its price. But I did want to say that I was . . . pleasantly surprised."

Ness smiled humorlessly. "The *Call and Post* has made me, and my department, out to be heavies. The editor, who I believe is on your board, likes to link my name with charges of police 'terrorism' and 'brutality.' "

"You've been criticized," Hollis admitted. "With some justification, I'm afraid."

"I don't see it that way."

Hollis cleaned his glasses on a white hanky; his expression was pleasant, his tones warm, but his words had bite.

"When Negro bathers were being harassed at Woodland Hill Pool this summer," he said, "you withdrew the two Negro policemen who took the white bathers to task. When park police used their nightsticks on a Negro couple at Euclid Beach for no reason other than race, you stood behind your men. Similarly, you failed even to reprimand the officer who shot and killed a fifteen-year-old boy, in the disturbance the night Joe Louis defeated Schmeling."

Ness did his best not to sigh. He said, with as much patience as he could muster, "Reverend Hollis, I am not the chief of police. You're speaking of matters that are not under my direct supervision."

"That sounds suspiciously like passing the buck, Mr. Ness."

"Perhaps. But I back Chief Matowitz in his decisions. As I understand these situations, Chief Matowitz responded responsibly."

"That's your view, sir?"

"Yes. Those officers were withdrawn from Woodlawn Hill Pool in an effort to cool off a racially tense situation. The couple you say were assaulted by park police were resisting arrest, for drunk and disorderly conduct. And they were convicted."

"I see. You assume that the Negroes were lying."

"If by that you're implying race prejudice on my part, I should point out that *you're* assuming the white cops were lying. It cuts both ways, Reverend. And the Joe Louis victory 'disturbance' you refer to, as you well know, was a full-scale riot that tore the entire Central-Scovill district apart."

Hollis shifted uneasily in his wooden chair. "It was a celebration that got out of hand. Tragically out of hand. A fifteen-year-old boy died, shot in the back."

"That *is* a tragedy," Ness said, meaning it. "I'm told the policeman was firing warning shots into the air, but got jostled. Bricks were being hurled at him. Four policeman were hospitalized, Reverend. A tragic night indeed; but not an example of rampant police brutality."

Hollis had a somber expression that stopped short of a frown. "It was obvious that the focal point of any Louis victory celebration would be East 55th and Central. Why didn't you detail more policemen, to prevent these things?"

Ness shook his head in exasperation. "And then be accused of subjecting the east side to undue force? Reverend, how exactly can I win with you?"

After an awkward moment, a chagrined smile spread across the preacher's face. "Mr. Ness, I believe I may have misjudged you in the past. You 'won' with me last week, at the market, let me assure you."

Ness smiled politely, glanced at his watch. "Reverend, I really do have another appointment. If I can be of specific help . . ."

"Mr. Ness, I think you know of the goals of the Future Outlook League."

"I do, and I agree with them. You're trying to persuade white-owned businesses in Negro neighborhoods to hire Negro help."

Hollis sat forward. "It's that, Mr. Ness, and more. We also advocate Negro ownership of businesses in those neighborhoods. That's why I am so encouraged, when I read in the white papers that you have made as your next target the Italian gangsters who hold the east side in their sweaty grip."

Ness might have been amused by the preacher's arch phrasing had the sincerity of the words not been so deep. But he failed to see the connection between his attack on the Mayfield gang–ruled numbers racket and the F.O.L. advocating home-owned businesses. He told Hollis that.

Hollis replied, "Before the Italians moved in, the policy and clearing-house business was a positive economic force on the east side. Men like Rufus Murphy contributed to charity, to churches, but even more important, they invested their money in Negro businesses."

"I'm afraid, Reverend, that I still do not see your point."

"I'm suggesting that the numbers game is a harmless diversion for my race, and one that provides many desirable economic side effects."

"It's not so harmless when you start listing the corpses that have accumulated in the past five years."

Hollis raised a finger. "That is not the doing of the Negro

policy kings. That was a one-sided war. The Italians did all the shooting."

"That would seem to be true," Ness admitted.

"Frankly, Mr. Ness, you have a problem. You will need the evidence of the Negro numbers operators, who are now reluctantly aligned with Black Sal Lombardi."

"That is definitely true."

"How do you propose to gain their trust, their support?"

Ness pointed at himself with a thumb. "I'll offer police protection. I have a reputation for protecting the lives and even the identities of my witnesses. If you followed my investigation into illegal labor practices, you'll know that's true."

Hollis was smiling again, the frustrated smile of a man trying to explain a complexity to a child. "You must understand, Mr. Ness, that the Negro numbers operators are going to be . . . reticent about cooperating with you, as they are technically law-breakers themselves."

"No 'technically' about it. But I'm prepared to offer immunity in return for testimony."

"Then I am prepared to help you. To act as an intermediary with the colored community."

Ness leaned forward. "You are? Reverend Hollis, that would be most appreciated . . ."

"But I would need to be able to pass along certain assurances."

"What sort of assurances?"

"That the policy and clearing house games will be turned back over to the Negro community, once we've helped you drive the influence of the Italian gangsters out of our neighborhoods."

"You mean . . . exercise a sort of benign neglect, where the numbers racket is concerned, once it's back in Negro hands?"

Hollis nodded somberly.

Ness frowned. "Reverend Hollis, I'm disappointed that a

man of your stature, of your religious background, would even suggest such a thing."

Hollis seemed both sad and amused. "Mr. Ness, policy is not a crime, on the east side. It's a small ray of hope, in one sense. In another, it's a rare example of economic independence for my people. There are others of 'stature' in the Negro community who feel as I do."

Ness knew that Hollis meant Raney and the other Negro councilmen, who would certainly like to have the campaign contributions of the policy kings once again.

Wearily, Ness rose.

He said, "Thank you for stopping by, Reverend."

"Will you think it over, Mr. Ness?"

"I have," Ness said. "No deals."

Hollis smiled patiently. He rose and said, "Life is more complicated than that, Mr. Ness. Consider it. Ponder it. My offer stands. Good afternoon."

He nodded and Ness held open the hall door for the man, and let him out. Hollis's footsteps echoed out on the marble floor, sadly, ominously.

Detective Albert Curry passed the clergyman on the walkway and met Ness, who was getting into his topcoat, at the office door.

"Wasn't that that fellow Hollis? From the Negro protest group?"

"Yes," Ness said, locking his office door.

"What did he want?"

"To protest," Ness said. "Let's take an unmarked car, Albert. We'll leave EN-1 in the parking lot."

Curry nodded and followed Ness onto the open hallway; beyond the railing the City Hall atrium rose. "Moeller and the others are waiting at the station," he told Ness.

"Fine," Ness said.

A few minutes later, Curry was behind the wheel of a black Ford sedan.

"Where did we get this tip?" Curry asked, driving.

"Garner."

"Already? He hasn't been undercover a week!"

Ness shrugged. "He's good at it. Struck up a friendship with one of Frank Hogey's policy runners."

Curry smiled over at his boss. "He's the biggest policy banker on the east side. And the only white one."

Ness said nothing for a while, watching the downtown glide by his window. Then he said, "Hogey knows his way around the legal system. Used to be a Police Court bondsman. But if we make a good bust . . . maybe we can do some business."

Soon they pulled up the ramp into the parking lot of Central Police Station at 21st and Payne, where they met Sergeant Moeller and two rookie patrolmen, who wore plainclothes for the occasion. Ness had requested that Moeller pull in two rookies, because Ness had virtually hand-picked every cop added to the force since he'd taken the safety director job. He could trust rookies.

They took two unmarked cars, taking 22nd less than a mile down to Central Avenue. Off Central, on East 36th Street, in the slum-choked midst of the Central-Scovill district, was a run-down, wooden-frame house, the paint long ago having peeled off it, a big ungainly structure with a short front yard thick with dead weeds. The two cars rolled down the street, windows down.

It was dusk already, though it was not yet six; the smells of pungent cooking spiced the air. All of the houses here were large enough to serve several families, but were ramshackle enough to topple in a strong wind. A few colored school kids were running down the sidewalk, playing a game Ness didn't recognize and laughing for no reason Ness could discern, other than childhood itself. He envied them their innocence, but not their future.

As they had prearranged, the car with Moeller and the two rookies parked on East 36th, just down the block from the house in question. Ness and Curry drove around back, to the alley, where they parked and got out and skirted a tumbledown shack of a garage and walked quietly across the backyard, where a dead dog was rotting next to a discarded mattress, to the rear of the house, where on the back steps a man and a woman, both colored, were smoking and laughing.

The man, who might have been twenty, wore a dark gray suit with wide pinstripes and wide lapels and a dark tie with a jewel stickpin; he wore black and white shoes and looked as spiffy as a department store mannequin. The woman, who was probably five years older than the man she was sharing her cigarette with, had skin the color of copper and her slinky, clingy dress was of a shade only slightly darker than her own. She also wore black high heels and a choker of cultured pearls and her hands flashed with jewelry.

They looked at the two approaching white men with suspicion, nostrils flaring, but held their ground.

"You the man?" the man asked.

Ness knew what the question meant and answered it by opening his coat to reveal his gold "City of Cleveland—Director of Public Safety" badge, which he'd pinned to his suitcoat lapel before leaving the office.

The man raised an eyebrow and cocked his head. "You *the* man."

Then without being told, he raised his hands, and Curry patted him down.

Curry looked at Ness. "Clean."

The girl, attractive and wide-eyed if a little hard, said, "You're Eliot Ness?"

"Yes," Ness said, moving up the rickety steps. "If you'll excuse us, please . . ."

And he moved past them, Curry on his heels. The back door opened directly onto a good-size kitchen, where aromatic pots steamed on a coal-burning stove. A heavy-set black woman in her fifties in an apron over a housedress was tending the pots, while at a beer bottle–littered kitchen table two black men in shirtsleeves and shoulder holsters sat playing cards.

"Guns on the table and not a sound," Ness said quietly.

The two men froze for a moment, then dropped their cards

before them, and carefully withdrew their revolvers, setting them on the table like a cautious bet they were making.

Curry collected the guns, dropping one each in an overcoat pocket; then he had the men stand, cuffed them together, and cuffed one of them to a water pipe near a Hoosier cabinet.

Ness did not wait while Curry did this, but went on up the back stairs, which were to the left of the door as you came in. The narrow, dark stairway rose to a small landing.

He knocked sharply, said "Police," and then kicked the door open.

A dozen people, all but one of whom were colored, were in the center of the large, largely unfurnished room, gathered around a big wooden table where eleven adding machines were being used to tally up the day's take. Adding-machine tape curled in snakelike coils on the table. On the floor nearby were two steel trunks brimming with thousands of betting slips. A short fat safe squatted in one corner.

They all seemed stunned by Ness's presence, their fingers still poised at their adding machines. All but the white man—Frank Hogey—were seated. A generally well-dressed lot, ten men and two women, they were essentially accountants and Ness—who had worn no gun to the raid—felt no threat from them.

"Stay right where you are," Ness said. "Nobody's leaving."

Hogey, a genial, stocky, balding man in his early forties, wearing a brown suit, a red tie loose around his neck, said, "There'll be no trouble, Ness. Don't worry. My boys behave."

At that moment, a razor-thin man in tortoise-shell glasses and a natty suit and tie bolted from the table and headed for the door, pushing past Ness, who reached out and grabbed him by one arm. The guy swung at Ness, and Ness ducked, losing his grip on him.

"Now, Junior," Hogey was saying in the background.

Junior, his eyes wide behind the glasses, reached under his shoulder under his coat and came back with a snubnose .38.

"I ain't goin' back to jail, Mr. Hogey. Not for you nor nobody."

With Junior's eyes on Hogey, it seemed a good time to grab that gun, which Ness started to do, when Junior turned his gaze back on Ness and pointed the gun forcefully, meaningfully at the detective.

"Back off," Junior said.

And he backed out of the room out onto the landing.

Then, for no apparent reason, framed in the doorway, still facing them, Junior crumpled to the floor and lost his balance and slid down the back stairs, clatteringly.

Curry stepped in from the landing. He'd been standing to one side of the door out there. His face was bloodless. He was holding his revolver by the barrel, having used the butt to club Junior.

"I hope I didn't kill him," Curry said.

Ness smiled gently. "Why don't you check and see. And get Moeller and the rookies up here. We've got some arrests to make."

Then Ness turned to Hogey and said, "Why don't you open that nice little safe over in the corner, Frank? Let's see what your take was today. . . ."

The take had been twenty-five thousand dollars.

In the papers it would be called, accurately, "the biggest haul in Cleveland history against the numbers racket."

And policy king Frank Hogey had been nailed but good; caught on the premises with evidence to spare.

In an interrogation room at Central Police Station, Ness spoke to Hogey about this and more.

"We have you, Frank."

Hogey, seated in a hard wood chair, one leg crossed casually across the knee of the other, said cheerfully, "It would seem so."

"You're going to jail."

"Possibly."

"Unless, of course, you don't want to go to jail."

"Ness. Spit it out. What are you trying to say?"

Ness shrugged. "I'm saying that you used to be your own boss. You used to be the most powerful policy king of the east side."

"I still am."

"No. You're a glorified stooge, and not all that glorified. You're a traffic cop between the Italians and the coloreds. And you know it."

The mask of geniality slipped a bit; his cheek twitched and he said, "I do all right."

"You could do better."

Hogey's face showed no interest.

Ness pressed on anyway. "You testify against Lombardi and Scalise, and I'll arrange immunity for you. On this charge, and on anything else that comes out in the numbers investigation."

Hogey's eyes glazed over. "I don't think so."

"Why don't you think it over, Frank. Talk to your lawyer about it."

He snorted a laugh. "You're dreaming, Ness. Nobody's gonna stool on the Mayfield boys. You ain't gonna get no help on this. You're all alone."

"Frank, you're wrong. When people start talking, and I start putting the 'boys' away, you're going to wish you'd gotten on my team while there was still time."

"I don't think so. Who's gonna talk? Hell, you can't get to *me* and I'm *white,* for Christ's sake. You think the jigs are gonna talk to you?"

Hogey began to laugh. His laughter bounced off the walls of the small interrogation room.

"See you in court, Frank," Ness said, but Hogey only laughed more.

Ness closed the door on the cubicle and nodded to the cop on duty to haul Hogey to the lock-up.

He met Curry in the hallway.

"Any luck?" he asked Curry, who had been interrogating the Negroes arrested on the raid.

"None," Curry said. "Oh, that guy who made a run for

it—Junior—he had an outstanding burglary rap; broke his collarbone, incidentally. How about you? You have any luck with Hogey?"

"I'd have done better," Ness said with a sigh, "betting a buck on the numbers."

It was now nearing ten. Ness decided it was time to think about supper. That might remove the gnawing feeling in his gut.

But somehow he didn't think it would.

7

Past midnight, on a Thursday night, in a black business district on Carnegie, not far from the east side market, Angelo Scalise exited the alley next to the Elite Cabaret, wiping the blood off his hands with a hanky. The night was dark and cold and not a soul was on the street; but the Elite was open, and so was the restaurant next door, Pig Foot Heaven, out of which came smells so foul Angelo thought he might puke. A few other storefronts were open on these couple of blocks; several bars, a barbecue stand, and a barbershop–numbers drop, where the "hep cats" paid to get their kinky hair straightened ("conked") by a mixture of Vaseline and potash lye.

In a black tailored suit with a black shirt and white tie and a black fedora with white band, Angelo looked as dapper as a zoot-suited Negro pimp. But he would have hated to hear that comparison: He had only contempt for "niggers." The only thing he liked about niggers was their money. The dumb monkeys were poor as piss ants but they gambled every damn day of their life, trying to hit that lucky number. He laughed to himself, wadding the bloody handkerchief, kneeling at a nearby steaming sewer grating, where he dumped it. He stood and lit up a cigarette and smiled.

A couple exited the Elite, dressed to the teeth. The man, a big, chiseled-featured Negro of fifty-some years, wore a camel-hair topcoat, under which flashed a yellow silk shirt and a dark blue tie; he had fingers full of jewelry—the gaudiest example being a heavy gold signet with a ruby, which was his lodge ring—but the woman on his arm was equally expensive. A "high-yellow gal" in buffalo-fur coat under which could be glimpsed a low-cut dress as pink as Pepto-Bismol. Her high heels clicked on the pavement. Both man and woman were bathed in neon, the man's dark complexion and her lighter one turning strange decorative shades.

The man was Willie "the Emperor" Rushing, one of the policy kings that Angelo and his cousin Sal had moved in on, five years ago. Willie resented the Mayfield gang—of that Angelo had no doubt—but the Emperor was their boy, now. With the expansion beyond the black district that the Mayfield gang had encouraged and made possible, Willie—even with kicking back 40 percent to Lombardi and Scalise—was still making good dough. Not what he had in the old days, Angelo realized; but Willie was alive and well, which was more than Rufus Murphy and dozens of others other could say—if dead niggers could talk.

Willie and his woman stood at the curb; they were waiting for a taxi or their driver, Angelo supposed. Willie was whispering in the giggly girl's ear; she was drunk or hyped on something. Angelo cleared his throat.

Willie looked over sharply; his eyes were as penetrating as knife blades. But his face softened into an insincere smile on seeing Angelo.

"Mr. Scalise," he said, abandoning the girl and walking toward Angelo. The way he said "mister" made it sound like "mist."

"Willie. Out for a big night? Is that your new wife?"

"I ain't married yet, Mr. Scalise." Willie's smile was an ivory gash in his charcoal face. The Emperor had been married four times, each time to a showgirl like this yellow bitch undoubtedly was.

"What's the latest on these Pittsburgh boys, Willie?"

Willie shook his head. "Like I tol' you on the phone, Mr.

Scalise, they is cutting in on our business something fierce. We oughta do something."

"We will. You been approached?"

"Me?"

"You."

Willie thought about that; tasted his tongue. Then he smiled and said, "Yeah, I was havin' a talk with 'em just this evening. I tol' 'em they could put their money where the sun don't shine."

Angelo smiled; he patted the older man on the shoulder and said, "You're a good boy, Willie." The Emperor's face tightened, just barely, around his eyes.

Then Willie said, "The one you oughta talk to is name of Rosato."

"Rosato. Yeah. So I hear."

"He's the turkey you're after, Mr. Scalise."

Angelo gestured with his cigarette in hand, toward the nightclub behind them. "Hangs out here, I hear."

"Yes, sir. He in there now."

"So you were just talking to him."

"That's right."

"You didn't mention that."

"I said they was coaxin' me this evening, Mr. Scalise."

Tension was pulled tight as a wire in the nighttime quiet. A cat yowled and broke the moment.

Angelo smiled. "So you did, son. So you did."

Willie smiled synthetically and said, "Got to get back to my woman."

"I wouldn't mind a taste of that little biffa myself."

Angelo had just referred to the woman as a whore, in street parlance.

"She ain't that kind of gal, Mr. Scalise," Willie said, quietly. He wasn't smiling now.

Angelo shrugged. "No offense, Willie. Hey, here's your cab. Don't miss it."

A yellow cab had just rolled up. Willie nodded and turned to join his antsy high-yellow gal and Angelo called out to him gently, "Don't worry about those Pittsburgh punks, Willie. By morning they'll be yesterday's news."

Willie had an arm around the girl's fur-clad shoulder; she was as jumpy as a facial twitch. Willie flashed his ivory grin and said, "Hope so, Mr. Scalise. Them odds they're givin' is givin' us fits."

The Emperor held the back door open for his woman, who got in, flashing a well-turned calf in a silk stocking. Yes indeed, Angelo thought, I'd certainly like a taste of that. Angelo's prejudices had their limits.

Angelo sauntered into the low-ceilinged, modern bar. Pale copper wall lighting stained the tables where flashily attired patrons, black and white and many a shade in between, sat smoking, drinking, chatting. Smooth hustlers with conked hair sat playing sex games with their yellow chorus-girl bitches, whose faces were powdered ghost-white, long lacquered nails redder than blood, full mouths bruised a similar red. Blue-gray smoke streams twisted upward lazily through the murkily lit room, blending with the smell of whiskey, perfume, and sweat. The bandstand was empty, but the jukebox was pounding out Count Basie's "One O'Clock Jump," and some couples, black and white, were cutting up a rug. Angelo didn't mind the music—you couldn't keep your damn toe from tapping to that jungle shit—but he didn't like seeing whites and coloreds mixing like that; but at least the whites were dancing with whites and blacks with blacks. Still, all in all, this old world was going to hell in a hand basket.

This was one place where policy racketeers of both colors, and anybody with money and the inclination, could mingle. But it was not the kind of place where Angelo would go for any reason but business. Eyes flickered his way, though not obviously, as Angelo moved toward the circular mahogany bar. He ordered a whiskey and surveyed the room.

Johnny Rosato was seated at a corner booth with two of his cronies. They were parleying with a colored kid named Freddy Douglass. Douglass was a slickly dressed young man who worked for Frank Hogey, or anyway had, before Hogey got shut down, at least temporarily, by that bastard Ness.

Douglass was (though of course Angelo did not know it) the man who had been standing talking to his girlfriend on the back steps of the house Ness had raided earlier that week.

The four men had apparently not noticed Angelo come in, caught up in their own wheeling and dealing.

Angelo finished his whiskey, waved off the black-uniformed bartender's offer of another. All of Angelo's drinks here were on the house, of course. He had much the same privileges as a cop.

He walked cockily over to Rosato's table. Douglass caught first sight of Angelo, and his eyes were large and white in his dark face. *Feet do yo' stuff,* Angelo thought, and laughed to himself.

Rosato, a heavy-set, nattily dressed man of about twenty-five, looked up at Angelo, blankly.

"You want something?" Rosato asked, with bland menace.

The other two, also well-dressed, a skinny kid of perhaps twenty with pockmarks and a short, sallow, dead-eyed hood, looked at Angelo with immediate contempt. None of them—except Douglass—recognized him.

"Mr. Scalise," Douglass said, nervously, starting to get up. "I was just havin' a friendly drink . . ."

The white men at the table did their best to show no reaction to the name "Scalise"; all of them, to one extent or another, failed, although the dead-eyed one did the best job of it.

"Go over to the bar, Freddy," Angelo said. "I want a private word with these gents."

"Sure thing, Mr. Scalise," Freddy said, and climbed out of the booth quick as a rabbit.

"Freddy," Scalise said, without looking at him. "Don't leave the premises. Stick around."

"Sure thing, Mr. Scalise," he said, and was gone. Jesse Owens couldn't have beat him to the bar.

"Have a seat, Scalise," Rosato said.

Scalise pulled up a chair and sat facing all three men. He said, "Ain't they heard of respect in Pittsburgh?"

Rosato's round face was impassive. "What's that supposed to mean?"

"It means most people call me 'Mr. Scalise.' It means you shoulda come callin' on me and Mr. Lombardi and paid your respects before setting up shop in our town."

Rosato smiled faintly. "My apologies, Mr. Scalise. But I wasn't aware this was anybody's town. I thought this was America. In America a man can do business where he likes."

Now Scalise smiled. The two bodyguards, or whatever the fuck they were, were staring at him. "This isn't America. This is Cleveland. In Cleveland, you want to check in with Mayfield Road before you get into business."

"We don't see it that way. We think an open market is the American way. You and your cousin, you want to compete, then give your customers better odds. It's that simple."

Angelo carefully took his cigarettes out of a side suitcoat pocket. He shook one out, tapped it on the tablecloth, and lit it. A smile lit up around it. He said, "Nothing is simple on the east side, Mr. Rosato. But I can make life a little less complicated for you."

"Oh?"

Angelo shrugged. "If you want to kick back forty percent of your take to us, we'll consider overlooking the lack of respect, the sense of common old-world courtesy, that you boys seem short on."

Rosato's pleasantness dropped away like the facade it was. He leaned forward and spoke through clenched teeth. "You Mayfield Road boys are soft. Second-generation pussies. Inherited the family business from your daddies. Where I come from, we make our own way."

"Really?"

"You bastards are getting eaten up alive by that Boy Scout Ness. You're not on top of things. The ground is falling out from under you. We, on the other hand, we're sitting pretty."

Angelo said nothing; his face was devoid of expression; his eyes were placid. He exhaled smoke.

That seemed to unnerve Rosato a bit—which it was supposed to.

With a magnanimous wave of the hand, Rosato said, "We're not telling you to shut your action down. We feel there's room in the marketplace for competition. Maybe we can both have a slice of the pie. Maybe the best man will win. That's the American way . . . Mr. Scalise."

Angelo thought about that.

Then he said, "Would you agree to raise your odds to the accepted 600 to 1?"

Rosato did a poor job of suppressing a smile; obviously, he felt Angelo was showing his weakness already. But Rosato responded, toughly businesslike: "What would be in it for us?"

"You wouldn't have to raise 'em right away. But once you're established, you'll have your customers. Why waste the honey, once you attracted all the fucking bees you need?"

Rosato thought about that. "And there'd be no trouble between us?"

"Well," said Angelo, with a winning smile, "my cousin won't like it. But he trusts me. He listens to me. I could swing it, yeah."

Rosato laughed shortly. "For a price, you mean."

"For a price. Not a piece of the action: a flat fee of ten grand."

Rosato glanced at the dead-eyed man, who—a beat later—shrugged.

"That might be possible," Rosato said.

"And if you needed anything smoothed out," Angelo said, "you could come to me. In some cases, what the hell—I'll do you a little favor, out of friendship. Other times, it might cost you a little."

"That could get out of hand. . . ."

"It won't. You got Angelo Scalise's word. But I don't want you to deal with me direct."

"Who, then?"

"There's a colored guy who works for me name of Leroy Simmons. He'll be our contact."

Rosato smiled at the dead-eyed guy, who actually cracked a smile. So did the pock-marked kid.

"Are you sure about that?" Rosato said, with smug amusement. "We recruited him tonight—not an hour ago. Right in this very club."

"I know," Angelo said, easily. "I ran into him outside. I told him to wait."

Rosato drew back. "Wait? What in hell for?"

Angelo laughed. "I knew what he was doin' here. It's all over the east side that you gents are holdin' court here. When he saw me, well—afraid I scared him shitless."

"Is that right?"

Angelo gestured open-handedly. "I thought we might . . . work something out. Between gentlemen. So I 'recruited' Leroy myself. Let's go out and talk to him."

The three men exchanged wary glances.

Rosato said, "Why don't you go out and invite Leroy in?"

Angelo frowned. "Are you fuckin' nuts? I don't want the three of us seen together." He meant Rosato, Leroy, and himself; he was excluding Rosato's goons in the head count.

"I don't like it," Rosato said.

"Hey—*paesan*. I'm not packin' heat, okay? You wanna frisk me when we get out there? Go ahead. I'm alone. You can bring your boys, I don't give a fuck."

Rosato drew a slow breath. Then he and his goons exchanged glances again and Rosato shrugged, to himself more than them, and said, "Okay. Let's go see Leroy."

They abandoned the booth and left the club, Angelo taking the lead in his sauntering way.

The night was chilly, but none of the men wore topcoats. Rosato and his boys had left theirs in the club; and Angelo had left his elsewhere, too.

Rosato touched Angelo gently on the arm. "No offense— but I'm gonna take you up on your offer."

"What offer?"

"To let one of my boys frisk you."

"No big deal." Angelo shrugged, good-naturedly.

The dead-eyed sallow one patted Angelo down, then looked at his boss and shrugged. Rosato nodded to him, then nodded to Angelo and said, "Where's Leroy?"

"Step into my office, gents," Angelo said, gesturing to the alley.

Rosato and his boys again traded glances, but they followed Angelo into the dark alley. They outnumbered him three to one, after all, and were armed and he wasn't.

"Where the fuck *is* he?" Rosato demanded, unbuttoning his suitcoat. The alley was claustrophobic and blacker than the east side and dead-ended at a row of garbage cans.

"Right here," Angelo said, and he took Rosato gently by the arm and pointed to Leroy, a small, handsome, sharply dressed Negro who was sitting between two garbage cans with his throat slit.

Rosato took a step backward as Angelo dipped down, plucked the switchblade from beside the corpse as the dead-eyed bodyguard moved forward. Angelo grinned and lashed out with the blade and cut the man across the throat. Those dead eyes opened very wide and a hand came up and gripped where he'd been slashed and blood streamed down and through his fingers in narrow red ribbons. He fell to his knees and his eyes were really dead when he flopped face-down on the cement near Leroy.

Rosato was moving backward and the other bodyguard was coming forward, the skinny pockmarked kid, yanking a gun from under his suitcoat and Angelo kicked him in the balls and when the skinny kid curled forward, gun dropping from his popped-open fingers, Angelo smacked him on the jaw, a good sharp smack that took the kid's legs out from under him. Then the kid was clutching his nuts, on his back like a dog scratching itself, and Angelo jammed the switchblade into the kid's stomach. The pockmarked kid began to gurgle, but never really made much noise at all.

The stunned Rosato was fumbling for a gun under his arm, but Angelo was on top of him, and pulled the suitcoat down around Rosato's shoulders, ripping it, pinning his arms, and hit Rosato in the forehead, violently, with his own forehead. The rush of pain felt just fine to Angelo.

Rosato was on his knees now, as if praying, or about to beg, which perhaps he was.

Angelo yanked Rosato's gun from its shoulder holster and stuck it in his own waistband and stood beside Rosato like a priest about to offer the host.

"I'm not going to kill you," Angelo said pleasantly. "Not tonight. If you're still in town tomorrow, you'll be deader than shit. Deader than your boys, deader than that nigger fink over there."

Rosato's whole face was trembling. "What . . . what do you want?"

"I want you to get the fuck outa Cleveland, what do you think I want, *goombah*? You wanna come back with some soldiers and play war, well, us second-generation pussies would just think that's dandy. That's the 'American way,' ain't it? Elsewise, all I wanna see is the ass-end of ya."

"What . . . what about . . . this?" Rosato's wide eyes made reference to the trio of bleeding corpses nearby.

Angelo shrugged. "A couple of Pittsburgh racketeers, who was far from home and in over their heads, got in a knife fight with a nigger policy runner. No big deal."

Rosato was shaking like a showgirl's behind; it was funny to Angelo. Funnier than fucking hell.

"We play this any different," Angelo said, "and the papers are gonna be full of gang-war bullshit, and Ness will be on all our asses. I got enough shit from that son-of-a-bitch already, so just go. Okay? Go."

Rosato, tentatively, rose. Angelo pulled the man's torn suitcoat back up around his shoulders, brushed him off as if he were Rosato's valet.

"Next time you're in town," Angelo said, walking him out

of the alley, an arm around the stunned Rosato's shoulders, "stop by Murray Hill and pay us your respects."

Rosato nodded numbly. He said, "I . . . better go in and get our coats."

"Yeah. You do that. The trains run all night, you know. I wouldn't waste no time. Shine killing or not, the cops might want to talk to you. Better to be missing."

Angelo walked him back into the smoky bar. The jukebox was playing some honey-suckle blues number and couples were dancing close. Close hell, Angelo thought; they're fucking, standing up. What was the world coming to?

He watched Rosato, tail tucked between his legs, collect the topcoats at the coatcheck window. Angelo's own topcoat was ruined; it was out in the alley, stuffed in one of the garbage cans, with Leroy Simmons's blood all over it.

When Rosato had ducked back out into the night, Angelo strutted over to the bar where Freddy Douglass was nervously drinking one Tom Collins after another.

Angelo put a hand on Freddy's shoulder and said, "Step out into the alley with me, son."

"Why, Mr. Scalise?"

"There's something I want you to see."

Angelo didn't intend to kill Freddy. This was for purposes of education.

And to get the word spread about who owned the east side. Cousin Sal was right: It was important to be respected.

8

"Eliot," Mayor Burton said somberly, "this is a matter of politics."

Ness hated to hear the mayor say that.

What had endeared the mayor to him—from their first meeting over two years ago, in this same lavish, high-ceilinged office hung with huge tapestries of the Western Reserve's Indian days—was Burton's pledge that Ness would be given "a free hand, without political interference."

Even so, there had been an element of politics in Ness's job from day one. Burton had run only nominally as a Republican, stressing his status as an independent, and his city council was badly factionalized. Ness had been brought in, amidst much press fanfare about the "G-man who got Capone," to clean up the corrupt police department—and he had to do it quickly enough to embarrass budgetary support out of that surly city council. And he had, and it had worked.

But Ness had made his lack of interest in politics, even his contempt for it, clear to Burton. And Burton had promised that no investigation would be tainted by political considerations.

And the Mayor, who as the years and elections went by had become less and less independent and more and more aligned with the Republican party, had at times become impatient with his apolitical safety director. When Ness threw his Burton-cultivated publicity value behind Frank Cullitan, a Democrat, running for re-election as county prosecutor, Burton said not a negative word. The mayor knew what a valuable ally Cullitan was to Ness; but Ness knew that this had nonetheless been an embarrassment to Burton.

Still, neither the mayor nor his safety director could ignore certain political realities. Hard times and tight budgets had made it necessary to create a slush fund to help support Ness's investigative work—a slush fund created by prominent merchants and industrialists and other city fathers.

On a few instances, these financial "angels" had presented Burton and Ness with a bill they dared not leave unpaid—notably last summer, hushing up the identity of the Mad Butcher of Kingsbury Run to keep from embarrassing a prominent Cleveland family. Ness had gone along with this, but had felt compromised ever since.

Nonetheless, Ness had great respect for Burton. A sturdy, wedge-shaped man in his early fifties, Burton had a broad brow and regular features and prematurely white hair; he cared little about his personal appearance and even now wore a fairly rumpled, off-the-rack charcoal suit and wrinkled blue tie. His dark-circled eyes gave him a vaguely unhealthy, even sinister look, but his smile was winning.

Lawyer, war hero, family man, Burton was a hell of a good mayor, and a hell of a good man. But he was becoming a hell of a politician, too, and that disappointed Ness.

"I understand this fellow Hollis came to see you," Burton said.

"Yes he did."

"And he offered to help you in your numbers racket investigation?"

"That's right."

"And you turned him down."

Ness shifted in the hard wood chair. "I didn't make a deal with him, if you call that 'turning him down.' He wanted an assurance from me that I'd allow the numbers racket to flourish on the east side, once it was back in Negro hands."

Burton thought that over; his black eyebrows under the white hair made for a sterner look than he possibly intended. But that look made Ness uncomfortable.

Nervously, Burton plucked a big black Havana from a wooden humidor on his massive oak desk; he fired up the cigar and waved it like a wand. "Well, what's your goal? To stamp out the numbers racket, or to dismantle the Mayfield Road gang?"

"The latter," Ness shrugged. "I'm not naive enough to think that the numbers racket is ever going to disappear from the Negro district."

"There are those," Burton said calmly, "who feel the numbers are a harmless diversion for a people who can use some hope in their lives. Betting a penny or two seems innocuous enough."

This line of reasoning bored Ness, who said, "I'm not interested in the morality or immorality of gambling."

Burton pointed with the cigar. "You're only interested in controlling the criminal element that illegal gambling necessarily attracts."

"Right."

"Just as you were never a supporter of Prohibition, when you were the country's most celebrated Prohibition agent. You were merely upholding the law, and attempting to curb the criminal gangs."

"Right. I'm not exactly a teetotaler myself, as you well know. Is there a point you're making that's eluding me, Your Honor?"

Burton sighed. "It's simply this: You know and I know that if we get rid of the Mayfield Road gang's influence over the numbers racket, we're not going to make a top priority out of cracking down on the Negro racketeers that take over."

"Well . . ."

"Eliot. In all honesty. In all frankness. In a practical manner of speaking . . ."

"You're right," Ness admitted. "We're not set up for it. Even if we wanted to, we don't have enough Negro cops to work the east side. In a practical manner of speaking, Negro numbers racketeers, in the wake of Lombardi and Scalise's downfall, will flourish—modestly."

"Then why didn't you accept Hollis's offer?"

"Because I can't go around cutting deals like that. And besides, I may *want* to crack down on the Negro numbers racket, at some time. If I could get some Negro cops on the force . . ."

Burton smiled ironically; flicked cigar ash into a brass tray. "Whose fault is that?"

Ness shifted in the hard wood chair again. "Well—mine, I suppose."

"You've read the editorials in the *Call and Post*. The editors think your high requirements for police department candidates are designed to keep Negroes off the force."

Ness shook his head, saying, "That may be an unhappy by-product, but it wasn't even vaguely my intention. Just because I want high school graduates . . ."

"You toughened up the Civil Service exam to where a *college* graduate could flunk the damn thing."

"Some do," Ness shrugged. "Only one hundred out of a thousand applicants pass. After all, I expect candidates who can handle the curriculum at our police academy—psychology, arrest procedure, criminal law, first aid . . ."

"Eliot, I admire your high standards—and considering how you've turned the sloppiest, most venal police department in the country into one of the best in the world, well . . . what can I do but commend you?"

Ness was bristling despite Burton's flattery. "Are you suggesting I come up with an *easier* test for Negro applicants? *That* sounds like race prejudice to *me*."

"No, no, no. All I ask is that you give Hollis and others like him some consideration. With the police brutality incidents we've had . . ."

Ness raised a finger. "So-called . . ."

Burton waved his cigar in deference. "So-called police brutality incidents we've had, we have a need—a political need, and a moral one—to accommodate these people."

Racial concerns were nothing new for Burton, of this Ness was well aware. Burton's 1935 mayoral campaign had been a success due to his putting together a coalition of minorities—Negroes included. And Burton had been publicly vocal in opposing segregation in local hotels and restaurants.

"I understand the moral need," Ness said. "But I don't see where politics enters into this." He spit out the word "politics" like a seed.

Painfully, Burton explained. "We have a state election coming up, Eliot. I know all about your disinterest in politics, but this has been in all the papers. Next month? Governor? State senators, state representatives? Elective offices? Sound familiar?"

"Do I really deserve this sarcasm?"

"God, yes! The three black city councilmen who are behind Hollis and, yes, are tied to the would-be Negro numbers racketeers are *Republicans*. Not only do they control the crucial swing vote that gets you your police department and fire department funds, they are key figures for rounding up the Negro vote in the state election."

"The colored vote has always gone Republican," Ness said. Archly he added, "I may not know politics, but I know that much. It's been that way since the civil war."

Burton was shaking his head. "Times are hard, and times are changing. The New Deal is turning a lot of Negro voters Democratic. And I need to help deliver the Republican vote in this state election, Eliot. It's important to me."

"To you?"

Burton's cigar had gone out. He seemed about to relight it, then settled it in the ashtray, folded his hands, and smiled at Ness. There was embarrassment in the smile.

"I'm giving serious consideration to running for senator, Eliot, in the next national election."

Ness hadn't seen this coming; it struck him like a blow.

"This would be your last term, then . . ."

"No. There'd be one more term as mayor—and this all assumes we'd win the mayoral race next year."

Ness smiled dryly. "I think we can we make that assumption—you're the most popular mayor in the city's history. That's why the powers-that-be are singling you out for greater things. And I don't blame them."

"That's kind of you, Eliot. But those 'greater things' are unlikely to happen for me, if I'm not able to deliver the vote. And without the support of key race leaders, frankly, I can't."

"I see."

"I'd consider it a personal favor if you did your best to accommodate Hollis and Councilman Raney and other race leaders—if you can do so without compromising your own principles."

Ness said nothing.

Nor did Burton, and Ness realized their meeting was over. He stood and the two men, the two friends, smiled warmly if wearily at each other across the massive oak desk, and nodded their goodbyes.

Ness walked down the hall to his office, where Bob Chamberlin and Albert Curry were waiting, seated at one of the conference tables.

"How did it go?" Chamberlin asked; he was in the process of lighting his pipe, his long legs crossed casually as he leaned back against the table. He was in suspenders and shirtsleeves.

"I'm not sure," Ness said. He sat on the edge of the conference table.

Curry said, "What do you mean?"

"His Honor would like us to cooperate with Hollis and any other race leaders who are willing to help. Just what the ramifications of that are, well . . ."

Chamberlin's little mustache twitched as he smiled. "You mean, Burton wants you to give the Negro racketeers a free ride."

Ness said nothing.

Curry said, "Why don't we worry about that later . . . like if and when we put the Mayfield Road boys out of commission."

Ness smiled faintly. "Good point, Albert."

Chamberlin blew out some pipe smoke and shrugged. "So we cooperate with Hollis. Let's set up a meeting between you and him."

"Good idea," Ness said. "Albert, could you arrange that?"

Curry nodded and went over to the phone on the desk.

Chamberlin said, "When are you going to start utilizing the handful of Negro cops we have at our disposal?"

"Very soon," Ness said. "I'm going to put Albert right on that. . . ."

"Mr. Ness," Curry said, his hand over the mouthpiece of the phone. He looked pained. "I've located Mr. Hollis."

"Good."

"Not really," Curry said. "He's in the lock-up at Central Jail."

"What?"

Curry shrugged facially. "He and his Future Outlook League buddies got busted. They were picketing the Woolworth's store on Central Avenue, for not hiring blacks. It got a little out of hand."

Ness sighed. He turned to Chamberlin. "Get him out. And the rest of his people."

"What if he's already been booked . . . ?"

"I don't give a damn. Tell Matowitz to spring him, and set up a meeting between me and Hollis, tonight, here at the office."

Chamberlin nodded, put out his pipe and tucked it away, got up, put on his suitcoat and topcoat, and went out.

Ness turned to Curry. "I want to talk to Toussaint Johnson."

"When?"

"Now."

Curry nodded. "I'll call over to his precinct house and see if I can get a line on where he is."

Soon they were riding in the EN-1 sedan, Curry at the wheel, Ness sitting broodingly as they abandoned the imposing granite structures of downtown Cleveland to head down East Ninth Street toward the vile east-side area nicknamed the Bucket of Blood. They turned onto Scovill Avenue, a nightmarish slum street that ran from 55th Street to 14th Street on the edge of the Negro district. Late afternoon was blurring into early evening and those neons and street lamps that weren't broken or burned-out smoldered in the twilight and helped make a world that was all too real seem unreal.

The Bucket of Blood was an urban swamp of squalid cold-water tenements, ramshackle warehouses, filthy junk yards, and rat-infested garbage dumps. Mangy dogs and cats scurried; white eyes in dark faces looked with suspicion at the sedan as it glided by like an apparition. It was a street where addicts, bums, and winos mingled with honest out-of-work laborers and kids who scampered down streets littered with garbage, broken glass, and dog shit. This sordid world, Ness realized, was Toussaint Johnson's beat.

The Boll Weevil Bar was on the corner of Scovill and 35th, next door to a nameless flophouse. The long narrow boxcar of a bar had an endless counter at left with a scattering of tables along the right; the floor was covered with soggy sawdust. A few neon beer signs glowed on the walls and provided most of what little light there was; the air was stale and smoky and rippled with the strains of a Fats Waller tune, "I Want a Little Girl to Call My Own," from a colorful jukebox squeezed in the far corner. Two burly bartenders were working the customers, and looked capable of serving up ball bats as well as brews. The bar stools were filled with weary working men and petty hustlers and a few hard-eyed whores. Most of the tables were taken, too, primarily by drunks sleeping on their folded arms.

At one of the tables, with his back to the wall, was a big, angular-featured Negro in a dark brown suit that looked slept-in and a black fedora that looked run-over by a car, or maybe a truck. He was drinking a beer without any apparent enthusiasm. His angular eyes had a sleepy look, but that was deceptive: They didn't miss a thing.

Ness and Curry, the only white men in the place, were given the once-over by perhaps a third of the clientele. A good proportion were drunk or didn't give a damn. The two detectives approached the big angular Negro, who sat alone.

"Toussaint Johnson?" Ness asked. "Detective Johnson?"

Johnson nodded. He rose and offered his hand. "Director Ness. Pleasure."

Ness shook the man's hand—it was a firm, dry grip that didn't try to prove anything, was just naturally strong. "This is Detective Curry. He's on my personal staff."

Johnson and Curry nodded at each other; they did not shake hands.

"Take a load off," Johnson said. "Buy you a beer?"

"Sure," Ness said.

Johnson got up and went over and got three beers at the bar. His suitcoat was open and the strap of his shoulder holster showed; the bulges of big guns were obvious under either arm. He was called by some "Two-Gun" Toussaint, Ness understood.

Johnson sat the three beers sloshingly down and the men each took one.

"Here's to crime," Johnson said, raising his glass.

"We'd be out of work without it," Ness admitted, and took a drink of the tepid beer.

"How'd did you find me?" Johnson asked.

Curry said, "Your desk sergeant said you usually stopped in here when you got off duty."

Johnson nodded. "It's a friendly little place."

"Unlike the Elite Cabaret," Ness said. "I understand you're working that case."

"Oh yeah."

"How do you read it?"

Johnson's smile was barely there. "Knife fights on this side of town ain't no big deal. Usually."

"Usually. Something unusual about this one?"

"Well, this has all three players windin' up real dead. Tw゜ got their throats cut, one got stuck in the belly. How's that happen, exactly? Does a fella who's got his throat cut up and stick another fella in the belly? Or does a guy gut-stuck waltz over and cut another fella's throat? How does that happen, exactly?"

"I don't think it could."

Johnson's smile widened, but showed no teeth. Calmly he said, "We found a topcoat in a garbage can."

"So I hear," Ness said.

"Had a label from some fancy haberdashery in Terminal Tower. A white man's topcoat, you ask me."

"Well, I am. Asking you."

Johnson nodded. "Blood all over the top part. Blood type matches one of the dead fellas—Leroy Simmons. Kind of a spurtin' pattern on the coat."

"Splashed there," Ness said, "when somebody's throat got cut."

"Exactly."

"What does it add up to?"

Johnson shrugged. "Adds up to the Pittsburgh boys has all packed up and gone home. The east side is Lombardi's again, and the odds on the numbers is back to 500 to 1. Is what it adds up to."

"I'd like that coat," Ness said. "Maybe we can track the owner."

"I could use some help at that," Johnson said, and sipped his beer.

"So could I. I've been checking up on you, Johnson. Your record is good. Damn good."

Johnson's smile flashed white, suddenly. "If I wasn't already on the force, you think I could get on?"

That stung Ness, and it was close to impertinent; but he had to give the man his balls for making the remark.

"Yes I do," Ness said. "You have a high school education, and you served in the war, and well. I'd like a hundred like you."

"Maybe you would," Johnson said. "That way the *Call and Post* might get off your ass."

Curry swallowed and looked at his boss. Ness was impassive for a moment, but then he laughed.

"You're so right," Ness said. "Are you interested in working with me, and my staff, on this numbers investigation?"

"I thought you'd never ask," Johnson said, smiling again, but not whitely.

"You have a personal stake in this, after all."

"Yes I do. You got a right to know this, Mr. Ness. I was a friend of Rufus Murphy, the policy king. Before I was a cop, I was a bouncer in a place of his. Anyway. He was shot right in front of my eyes. I'm sure it was Lombardi's doing, and Scalise. I swore over my friend's bleeding body I'd get those bastards."

"Why haven't you? You've been a cop all these years."

Johnson laughed; it was as explosive as it was brief. "Mr. Ness, before you started kickin' these crooked cops outa their cushy jobs, *nobody* was a cop in this town, badge or not. There was pressure and there was politics and there was a lot of money floatin' around up above me. All of that kept me from doin' anything about going after Murphy's killers. I was ordered off that case. I was told if I went near it, I'd be off the damn force."

"I'm surprised that stopped you."

"It didn't. I been talkin' to people for years. I know dozens of witnesses who could put those tally bastards behind bars. But I can't get nobody to talk in public."

"Are we still up against that? Is this a dead end?"

Johnson shook his head, no. "Not if we team up, you and me. Without me, you can't do it. You don't know who to talk to. You wouldn't know how to talk to 'em, if you *knew* who to talk to. I know. Who. And how."

"But you've known that for five years, and what has it got you?"

"Not a damn thing—except, I know where the bodies is buried. Better still, I know who knows where the bodies is buried. And with my street savvy, and you to back me up, we can find witnesses, all right.''

Ness's eyes narrowed. "My backing you up will do that?''

"It will. The east side may not love you, Mr. Ness, but they trust you to do what you say you'll do. They know you're not crooked. They know when you say you'll protect a witness, you'll protect a witness. That union deal proved that. Together, Mr. Ness, we can turn Mayfield Road into a goddamn parkin' lot.''

Ness grinned. "You come through for me, Detective Johnson, and you'll be the first Negro sergeant on the force.''

"I was hopin' for chief," Johnson said, deadpan. "But I'll settle.''

The two men shook hands again.

"You had supper?'' Johnson said, getting up. He shambled out of the bar, climbing into a rumpled brown topcoat as he did, and Ness and Curry followed him.

"No,'' Ness said.

Curry shook his head, no.

"They serve up a mean gumbo down the street,'' Johnson said, pointing with a thumb. The street was dark, now, neon standing out starkly in the night.

"What's gumbo?'' Curry asked.

"New Orleans dish, isn't it?'' Ness asked.

"That's right,'' Johnson said. "Made outa pork, chicken gizzards, okra, sweet potatoes, shrimp, spices, herbs . . . but Pappy's down the street has got a secret ingredient.''

"What's that?'' Curry asked.

"Goat testicles,'' Johnson said.

The two white men, whiter than usual, thanked the Negro cop for his offer but tactfully declined.

As they left in the EN-1 sedan, Ness thought he heard roaring laughter behind him.

9

Toussaint Johnson was well aware that Al Curry was ill at ease, riding around the colored east side in Johnson's used Chevy sedan. Johnson did nothing in particular to add to the young detective's uneasiness; neither did he do anything in particular to lessen it. Toussaint Johnson had spent going on forty years as a black man in a white-ruled world, and he didn't mind seeing any white man get a sample of what it was like to be the minority.

This was their first day on the east side, in their attempt to gather witnesses for Ness, and Johnson had met Curry's attempts at making conversation with polite but terse and sometimes sardonic responses.

"What's it like working this side of town?" Curry had asked, as the sedan bumped over the ruts of Scovill Avenue.

"Lively," Johnson had replied.

"How can these people stand living like this?" Curry had later asked, with no condescension and with considerable sympathy.

"Day a time," Johnson had replied.

So it had gone for a while, and now Curry had lapsed into a morose silence.

That was fine with Johnson. He didn't like conversation for the sake of conversation with anybody, color aside. His wife, Maybelle, was a chatterbox, God bless her, and he had learned how to have lengthy conversations with her without listening to anything she—or for that matter, he himself—said.

He lived with Maybelle and their two boys and one daughter in a white frame house in a mixed neighborhood off Hough Avenue, near League Park, where the Cleveland Indians had played till the Municipal Stadium was built a few years back. His son Clarence was the star quarterback at East High, and his younger son William was an honor student. Johnson felt no guilt about living in a better neighborhood than the colored citizens of the Roaring Third who he served and protected. But he didn't feel superior to those people. Just luckier.

He had grown up in Central Scovill, the Bucket of Blood his backyard. Actually, he'd been born in a small South Carolina hamlet, but had no memories of it; his father and mother had moved north shortly after his birth. His parents had worked as domestics, in the South, and in Cleveland, Papa had got work as a waiter at a chi-chi hotel called Wade Park Manor, while mama worked as a housekeeper-cook for a wealthy white family in Shaker Heights. Both were God-fearing folks and had a Booker T. Washington advance-through-hard-work way of looking at things.

Young Toussaint had learned to read in his own home—a cramped one-room apartment in Central Scovill, at first, and later the top half of a frame duplex—and his primers had been everything from the Bible to W.E.B. Du Bois. He'd attended predominantly black Central High School and got high marks.

But Toussaint Johnson had never completely been able to buy into the Booker T. Washington philosophy. It sounded good on paper, but he saw too many folks of his race struggling and getting nowhere, his parents among them. What finally turned things around for Papa and Mama was when Papa won ten bucks in a dice game in the basement at the hotel, played it on 714 on the "money row" and hit for five thousand dollars.

Papa and Mama had then opened a little restaurant called Pappy's on Scovill and did very well after that—until Papa got robbed and killed in the restaurant, late one night just before closing.

Mama died the year after that. They called it a heart attack, but Toussaint knew that nothing had attacked her heart: It was flat-out broke in two.

What Toussaint Johnson had learned from all this was that life was a matter of luck, good and bad. But this was something he knew in his head; in his soul somewhere his mama had instilled enough of that Booker T. Washington work ethic that he kept trying hard, trying to get ahead, and his father's killing had given him a goal: He wanted to be a cop. He had seen the white cops dismiss his papa's murder as just another "shine" killing. And he saw that there was a need for good Negro cops in this bad Negro district.

The best place to get trained for that, he figured, was the army, and there was a war on, so he enlisted in Company D of the Ninth Battalion of the 372nd Regiment, Cleveland's all-Negro militia unit. He left his younger brother Edward to take the restaurant over, and soon found himself in France in combat.

Even in the army, even in a black company, the white man's influence prevailed. Their Negro commanding officers, Major John A. Fulton and Captain William Green, fine leaders, were relieved of duty and discharged as "physically unfit" before the company was sent overseas. Maybe if they'd been left in charge, Johnson often thought, Company D wouldn't have lost so many men. Johnson, like the other Company D survivors of the Argonne, came home wounded, and a recipient of France's highest military medal, the Croix de Guerre.

One of Johnson's fellow Company D survivors was Eustice N. Raney, who'd been a few years ahead of Toussaint at Central High. While they weren't close friends, Johnson and Raney liked and respected each other. They had both basked in the glow of the heroes' reception Company D received, including a parade in downtown Cleveland. Raney, however, had gone on to law school, while Johnson had found himself in deep shit.

Toussaint's brother Edward had lost the restaurant in a dice game. Edward had sold the family house and headed out for parts unknown. Toussaint never saw his brother again.

This left the Company D veteran—like so many others—without a job and with few prospects for one. Within weeks his sense of being a survivor, of being a hero and on top of the world, had faded back into the reality of being a young Negro in an old, white world. He applied to the police department but was turned down. He kept re-applying with the same result, while working a variety of day labor jobs and, for half a year, shoveling coal at Republic Steel.

About the only good thing that happened in those days was meeting Maybelle, a waitress at Pappy's, which Toussaint had continued to frequent. She was a beautiful chocolate-brown talkative girl with a generous figure and a good sense of humor that even getting pregnant couldn't faze, particularly since Toussaint was amenable to marrying her.

By 1922 Johnson's Company D compatriot Eustice Raney was making a name for himself in the colored community; he had graduated law school and with the help of Negro businessmen and politicians got himself appointed the city's first black police prosecutor. Raney's backers included the east side policy kings, and he helped Toussaint Johnson and half a dozen other Company D vets get jobs with Rufus Murphy and others.

Johnson became a bouncer for a Murphy associate, Gus "Bunch Boy" Smith, at his gambling den on the second story of a house on Central Avenue. It was Johnson's job to collect the guns and shivs off players before they were allowed in, and to watch for police raids, pressing a loose nail in the door frame to blink the lights.

During this same period, Toussaint never stopped applying to the police department. He saw no irony in his situation, as certain rackets on the east side—the numbers in particular, gambling in general—seemed only technically illegal to him. He wanted on the force to nail evil bastards like the robber that killed his papa, like the con men that stole old people's money with words, like the muggers and purse-snatchers and other thieves who preyed on the innocent.

One day in 1927, Prosecutor Raney asked Toussaint to drop by his office at the Criminal Courts Building.

Raney, a stocky, pleasant-featured light-skinned Negro with sharp, dark eyes, had sat behind a big mahogany desk with his hands folded like a preacher. His smile was gentle and a touch self-satisfied as he said, "They tell me you apply to the police department about three times a week."

"They exaggerating," Johnson said. "Some."

"I want representatives of our race on the department. There are people in city government who agree with me. White people. And a hell of a lot of Negroes on the east side feel that way. We need Negro cops. You're going to be one of them."

"Good."

"You have a fine war record, and a high school education. Good grades, too. Why didn't you go to college, Toussaint?"

"Money."

"What about your family's restaurant?"

"Lost it."

"Oh. Well, your latest application is going to be approved. Needless to say, your affiliation with Mr. Rufus Murphy will come in handy."

"I ain't gonna roust Murphy . . ."

"You might on occasion, for appearance sake." Raney smiled slyly. "No, Toussaint, Mr. Murphy is a friend of mine and a campaign contributor. You'll still be working for him, in capacities that you and he will determine. This is the last you and I will speak of it, because there might be, in the eyes of some, a certain . . . conflict of interests."

"You won't take the fall," Johnson assured him, "if it comes to that. I'm willing to take the job and what comes with it."

"Good!" Raney stood behind the desk and smiled and the two men shook hands. In two days Johnson's application was officially accepted.

The years that followed had been rewarding ones, in just about every sense. With his cop's pay and certain compensations from Rufus Murphy, Johnson was able to move his wife and two kids to the white-frame house on Hough. And he had racked up an arrest and conviction record second to nobody in the crime-ridden Roaring Third. Commendations overflowed in his file.

The gravy train had slowed, though, when the policy kings got overthrown by those tally bastards from Murray Hill. Added to that was the pain and sorrow of losing Rufus Murphy, of having this second father shot right out from under his file-folder-full-of-commendations ass.

But now there was a chance for recompense. Now there was a chance, finally, to revenge himself on those white sons-of-bitches. Now there was a chance, finally, to start putting money in the bank again, maybe put his two boys in college, give them a shot at a decent life.

He'd gone to Raney's law offices just yesterday and the councilman, looking fatter and sassier but with the same sharp hard look in his eyes, had told Johnson to cooperate with Ness.

"Ness works for Burton," Raney said, "and the Mayor *needs* the Negro vote—both in the council and at the polls."

"Ness don't cut deals," Johnson said.

"I know he doesn't. But he did have a meeting with Reverend Hollis yesterday evening, and gave certain assurances to Hollis."

"What kind?"

"Ness told Hollis he couldn't promise he'd cast an entirely benign eye on the numbers racket, once it got back in colored hands. But he admitted that it would not be high on his list of priorities."

"That's 'bout as close to a deal as you can get out of Ness," Johnson admitted. "Mayor must've put the pressure on."

"I'm sure he did. You spoke to Ness yourself?"

"Yes—right before he talked to Hollis, 'pears."

"And?"

"Ness had plenty of time to ask me about my ties to the numbers kings—and didn't."

Raney beamed. "Good, good. With the seal of approval of both Ness *and* Hollis, you may find yourself some witnesses."

"Maybe. But the Mayfield boys killed three men the other night. Two white and a colored."

"So I hear."

"That send a message 'cross the east side that ain't easy to un-send."

Raney's smile disappeared and he said, "I have confidence in you, Toussaint."

"I have confidence in dry ammunition, councilman."

Now Toussaint Johnson and his white companion Curry were trying to put the designs of this unlikely coalition— Mayor Burton, Eliot Ness, Councilman Raney, and Reverend Hollis—into motion. They were walking into a Central Avenue poolroom called the Eight Ball.

Behind a squared-off counter at the left as you came in sat a chunky cueball-bald Negro wearing a green eyeshade, collarless white shirt, and black vest with a gold chain. He was perched on a high stool, like a frog who thought he was a prince, guarding the cash register like it was his crown jewels, overlording six pool tables arranged in pairs of three. Cones of light spread from hanging lamps, cutting the dark, smoky parlor geometrically. It was the middle of the morning and only a couple of the tables were in use.

Slippery Stevens, wearing a dark suit and a dark tie and dark glasses, looked like a blind skinny undertaker. He was practicing; he couldn't find many locals to play him, good as he was. Johnson and Curry stood watching as Slippery chalked up a cue, placed the cue ball on its marker, stroked smooth and broke the balls, scattering them like gamblers out the back door when a raid was coming down. Five dropped into pockets, and then Slippery ran the rest, balls clicking like castanets. It took about two minutes.

Curry was visibly impressed.

Slippery leaned against the table, chalking his cue; his smile was as crooked as he was.

"Toussaint, my man," he said. He said the name like *too*-saunt. "Who's the ofay motherfucker?"

Curry blinked. Johnson repressed a smile; he had a notion that this casual term—"motherfucker"—was new to the white boy—possibly the very idea it expressed was new to him. But Curry didn't seem offended—just surprised.

"He's the man," Johnson said.

"Hell, Toussaint—*you* the man."

"He's the man, too. And he's with me. Call him a mother-fucker again and you'll have to squat to take your next shot."

Slippery's smile vanished, then returned. "So what's up, gentlemens?"

"I'm surprised to find you here," Johnson said. "Heard you was out on the road these days."

"Got to be," Slippery said. "Got's to play where my face ain't my callin' card."

"They must know you in a lot of towns by now."

"That they do."

"Might be nice to settle down."

"That it would."

"You ain't been able to light in one place since the old days."

Slippery had been one of the most successful independent numbers operators on the east side, before the Italians moved in.

"That's a fact, Jack."

"Wouldn't it be sweet if them tally fuckers would take a hike."

"That it would."

"Like to help 'em?"

"Yeah, boss, and I'd like to hit my number for about ten grand, too."

"Didn't Scalise and Lombardi themselfs put the muscle on you, Slip? Way back when?"

"That they did. They done it personal. Lombardi watched and Scalise beat the ever-lovin', ever-livin' shit out of me."

"They say Scalise tossed acid in your face."

"That's a fact, Jack. Damn near blinded me."

And Slippery took off his glasses; Curry flinched on seeing the scar tissue around the man's eyes. Slippery was a handsome man, but his scars weren't.

"Good thing I seen it comin'," Slippery said, sliding the shades back on, "and shut my peepers. Or I'd done lost my only other money-makin' knack. Blind men shoot piss-poor pool, you know."

Johnson walked over close to Slippery; he put a hand on the man's shoulder. "We puttin' together a Grand Jury. We gonna boot them tally fuckers outa the Roarin' Third."

"You and what the fuck army?"

"Me and Eliot Ness," Johnson grinned.

Fifteen minutes of explanation later, Johnson and Curry were back in the Chevy sedan, driving to their next destination.

"Sounds like he might cooperate," Curry said.

"He will," Johnson said. "He hates them bastards much as me."

The next stop was a tenement that even by Scovill Avenue standards was vile. Three old men, wrapped in threadbare sweaters and frayed mufflers, sat in kitchen chairs on the sidewalk right up against the front of the dilapidated frame building; it was even money whether the building was propping up the old men or vice versa. It wasn't a cold afternoon, but was chilly enough, and the old men's breath rose like steam. Johnson and Curry entered the building and walked down a long, narrow, dark, urine-scented hallway, the only light coming from one hanging bulb. The walls were whitewashed, or had been once, before filth and obscene graffiti had taken over. Curry blinked at the sight of a gigantic phallus with a comic-strip speech balloon hovering over it, saying, "Fuk fuk fuk." Johnson, a literate man, was dismayed himself—kids couldn't spell for shit no more.

They climbed three floors of dark stairs, occasionally skirting a wino or necking teenagers, and Johnson banged his fist on a numberless door, three times. The door shook from the blows.

"I can't stop you," a ragged male voice from within said.

Johnson opened the door and Curry meekly followed; the white boy's eyes were as round and white as Stepin Fetchit's.

It was a small, one-room apartment with cracked plaster walls, against one of which was a faded red overstuffed sofa that was sprouting its springs. Against another was a battered steel bed, its white paint chipping away, its tattered blankets and dirty sheets mingling in an unmade pile, one of its two pillows greasy with hair oil. Nearby was a chest of drawers with a catalog substituting for one busted-off leg and a cracked marble top bearing a single-burner gas plate. Near that was a small square table stacked with dirty dishes, and under the table was a cracked porcelain washbowl and pitcher. The water source was a single tap down at the baseboard, with several feet of garden-type hose attached. A single drop light hung like a noose from the center of the cracked ceiling. In back a rusted potbelly stove crouched beside a wooden box of coal. There was no bathroom.

A skinny black man in a T-shirt and shabby dungarees, thirty-some years of age, stood in the center of the room, just under the hanging light, as if contemplating tying its cord around his neck. His eyes were muddy, his posture stooped, his greased-back hair the only remaining sign of the street-smart slick hep cat he had been not so long ago.

"The man," he said, hollowly, looking at Toussaint.

"Hello, Eli."

"Can't offer you nothin'. Nothin' to drink right now."

"We'll just sit, then."

Johnson motioned to Curry and the two cops sat on the shabby sofa; a spring jabbed Curry in the ass, and he moved quickly to one side.

Eli stood before them. He looked weak, but he wasn't shaking, and he wasn't tottering.

"Are you on the sauce, Eli?"

"No, sir."

"Stickin' anything in your arm? Up your nose?"

"No, sir."

"What are you doin', then?"

"Tryin' to get myself back on my feet, sir."

"Looking for work?"

"I will be, sir. Can't go back to numbers runnin', not in this town."

"I hear Scalise had some boys beat you up, while back."

"Yes, sir."

"Why is that, Eli?"

"I was diddlin' this little high-yeller gal."

"Ah. Dancer at the Cedar Garden nightclub."

"Yes, sir. They calls her Ginger. Mr. Scalise was diddlin' her, too. I didn't mind. That comes with the territory, don't it?"

"Seems to, Eli."

"But he minded me diddlin' her. They busted me up pretty good."

"What about the girl?"

"She left town. She went to Chicago town. I might look her up there, when I gets on my feet."

"Did Scalise do any beatin' on you himself, Eli?"

"Yes, sir, he did."

"Would you testify to that?"

"No, sir, I would not."

"What if you had immunity?"

"What's that, sir?"

Johnson told him.

"I likes the sound of that. But Mr. Scalise is a bad motherfucker. He'd kill a black man soon as look at him."

"That right there is a good reason to testify, Eli. You heard of Eliot Ness?"

"Sure."

"How 'bout Reverend Hollis, the Future Outlook League?"

"Everybody heard of Reverend Hollis."

Johnson patted the sofa cushion next to him. "Sit down with us, Eli. This is Detective Curry, from the office of Eliot Ness. We want to talk to you."

In the car, Curry said, "I think that fellow could clean up into a damn good witness."

"So do I."

"He'll talk, won't he?"

"If he don't kill himself first."

"Kill himself?"

"He been curled up in that rat-hole healing himself. From that beating. Scalise took his girl, took his pride. Some wounds don't heal over."

Their next stop was a yellow Victorian on 46th off Carnegie, just west of Central-Scovill. The neighborhood was just one small grade up from the nearby slum, and many of the houses—single-family dwellings intermingling with larger rooming-house buildings—were pretty run-down. But the house that belonged to John C. Washington, retired policy king, was well kept-up; it even had a picket fence to make it seem almost idyllic—and to separate it from its more ramshackle neighbors.

When Washington had bought this property years ago, this neighborhood was a real step up from the slums; but the slums had spread like a disease, though Washington's dwelling had remained immune, an island of relative affluence. In the last several years, some buildings of the nearby slum area had been, and continued to be, torn down, as the WPA housing projects inexorably took their place.

"Toussaint, you are always welcome here," Washington said warmly, ushering Johnson and Curry through the vestibule, past the second-floor stairs, into the living room.

The living room was a small but beautifully furnished affair, floral wallpaper, oriental rugs, fringed draperies, wood-and-cut-glass bookcase, fireplace, on the mantel of which were portraits of relatives as well as a large one of elaborately uniformed Marcus Garvey of Back-to-Africa fame. Through a wide archway was the dining room, another small but perfect room, with a long windowseat where potted plants sat near sheer drapes.

Dignified and well-spoken, Washington was a lanky, handsome man of fifty-some years; his skin was a dark, lustrous black, his hair short, his apparel immaculate and expensive—he wore a white shirt and blue silk tie with tiny white polka dots, an English-tailored suit and white-and-black shoes. He had a superficial air of culture and the faintest southern accent, hinting at his illiterate sharecropper roots.

"Please sit down, gentlemen," Washington said, settling himself in an overstuffed green chair with doilies on the arms. A standing lamp with a fancy fringed shade looked over his shoulder.

Johnson and Curry sat on a nearby divan.

"You look well, Johnny," Johnson said.

"Life is sweet," Washington said solemnly.

"It could be sweeter."

Washington gestured around himself. "How?"

"You could still be policy king."

He waved that off. "I'm retired from that field."

A small, beautiful mulatto woman in her late thirties floated in from the dining room. She wore a pink crepe dress with a pearl necklace and a floral brooch. A handsome woman with a big fine ass, Johnson thought; Washington's former-showgirl wife Velma.

There were no introductions; Velma knew Johnson, and Curry was regarded as an invisible man.

"Would you men like some coffee, or tea?"

Washington requested tea and Johnson said that would be fine, too. Curry added a nervous third to the tally.

When she was gone, Washington said, "I can anticipate what you're after, Toussaint—the good Reverend Hollis paid me a visit late last night."

"So you know the score."

"I always do. What good does rocking the boat do? I have no yearning to get back in that business. I have legitimate interests now—real estate, a few restaurants . . ."

"You might be livin' in a better neighborhood, if Lombardi and Scalise hadn't come along."

"I have a nice home."

"What'll this neighborhood look like in five years? Ten? You got a young pretty wife, Johnny."

Irritation creased Washington's smooth, seemingly unused face. "I can take care of myself and my wife, Toussaint."

"You and your bodyguards, maybe. Why does a man who ain't in the rackets no more still move about with bodyguards?"

Washington shifted in his chair. "Any successful businessman is at risk. We live and work in a community that has more than its share of risks. You know that better than most—you're in the police business."

"I think it's 'cause you a nervous man, Johnny. Nervous ever since Scalise beat the hell out of you."

"Toussaint . . . I invited you into my home . . ."

Mrs. Washington returned with a silver tray on which were three cups of tea and a small bowl of sugar.

"If anyone would like cream," she said, "I can oblige."

No one did. The woman picked up on the tenseness in the air, quickly and efficiently served the cups of tea around, and left with grace and haste.

Johnson sipped his steaming tea. "I think you're still afraid, Johnny."

Washington's tea sat on a coaster on the small table beside him. His face was as blank as a baby's.

"No denying it, is there, Johnny?"

Washington looked at the floor. He seemed to be trying to decide whether or not to get mad.

Johnson sat forward. "There's a goddamn good reason why you should testify. Reasons beyond the fact that you're gonna be safe. Reasons beyond the fact that it could pay off for you, financially."

Washington smiled humorlessly. "And what reason is that, Toussaint?"

"The best reason there is, Johnny. Revenge."

Washington thought about that.

"If black men wasted time revenging themselves on white men," Washington said finally, "where would we be?"

"Where are we now?" Toussaint Johnson asked.

· TWO ·

JANUARY 9–10, 1939

10

Normally on a Monday, with a City Council meeting coming up at seven-thirty, Ness would have stayed in his office and worked straight through. But it was Ev's birthday and he had promised her they'd have supper together at the boathouse; then he could drive back and catch an hour or so of the meeting, for appearance sake, and return for a quiet evening with her.

He first met Ev MacMillan in Chicago, seven or eight years before, when he was still heading up the Justice Department's prohibition unit in Chicago. Daughter of a prominent stockbroker, she was really just a kid then, a fresh-faced art student; and Ness—married at the time—had taken notice of the attractive girl, but nothing more.

Then, a little over a year ago, at the Michigan–Chicago football game at Ann Arbor, he ran into her and some chums of hers at the stadium. He and Bob Chamberlin were staying at the same hotel as Ev, and she and her friends joined them for dinner. She had flirted with him, and he repaid the compliment, and as the wine flowed, things got friendly.

But sobering news, by way of a phone call, interrupted the proceedings: Ness's mother had died that afternoon.

Even though their relationship was but a few hours old, Ev insisted on accompanying him back to Chicago—she lived there, after all; and the two of them, still a little drunk, shared a compartment together and he cried in her arms. The thought should have embarrassed him, sober, over a year later, but it didn't.

He had stayed in Chicago for several days tying up family loose ends, and doing some work on the Chicago aspects of the then-ongoing labor racketeering investigation. She had stayed by his side. Day and night.

And when it was time to return to Cleveland, she came with him—not to stay. Just to see if he was telling the truth when he whispered, "Cleveland is very beautiful during the wintertime." He didn't think she'd found it beautiful at all; gray, dirty Cleveland hardly suited her artistic sensibilities.

But Ness himself, apparently, did suit her; because she began applying for jobs on that very first visit. She was a gifted artist who had already illustrated several children's books for New York publishers, and he didn't have to pull a single string for her to land her job as fashion illustrator at Higbee's department store. A few months later, she moved to what she was inclined to call "the dullest, dirtiest city on earth."

Ev had no complaints, however, about the boathouse hide-away in posh suburban Lakewood. The boathouse, which belonged to one of the Burton/Ness financial "angels," was on Clifton Lagoon, the deepest mooring point on Lake Erie; the boathouse was in an exclusive subdivision with a private, guarded drive and high-tone occupants. Ness was probably the only non-millionaire of the bunch.

She had waited till after the November elections to move in with him; but there had been no direct talk of marriage. Apolitical though he was, Ness did not want to cause Mayor Burton any problems, nor did he want to endanger his own job. Cleveland was a conservative, predominantly Catholic community and Ness marrying for a second time would be viewed with disapproval by many a voter.

Setting up unmarried housekeeping together might seem dangerous in and of itself, but Ness was in so tight with the newspaper boys that the Ness/MacMillan cohabitation was unlikely to go reported. Even Jack Raper, who took catty swipes at Ness in his column from time to time, would look the other way on this one.

His first marriage, to the woman who had been his secretary back in his Chicago "untouchable" days, had not been an unhappy one, exactly; he still thought of his ex-wife with affection, and they kept in touch, though there had been no children. It had been the pressure of his profession—the long hours, the danger, and (Ness now realized) his reticence to speak about that—that had finally made their marriage come irreparably apart.

Usually, when he made this drive it was after dark; in the overcast winter late afternoon, the sky looked faded, like it was wearing out. The castle-like boathouse itself and the skeletal trees nearby were stark against the sky. Small but massive, the turreted structure rose two stories with a smaller, third tower-like story crouching on top; the lights were on in the tower, meaning Ev was at work. A half-story stone wall created a modest courtyard. The barrenness of this study in gray tones—gray sky, dark gray lacework of bare tree branches against that faded sky, darker gray stones of the castle itself—was made picturesque by the several inches of white on the ground. Only the cement ribbon of the road, yet another gray tone, broke the spell of the snow.

The breeze had some bite but he didn't mind, as he stepped out of the EN-1 Ford sedan, which he'd parked behind Ev's dark-blue Bugatti right in front. He paused to look at the frozen lagoon, white and gray and gray-blue stretching to the horizon. No yachts this time of year. The weather gave no special dispensation to the wealthy.

He hung his topcoat in the closet, and slipped out of his suitcoat, which he folded neatly over a chair near the stairs. The brown leather shoulder holster that he always wore was, as usual, empty; he didn't like to carry a gun, but when a gun was needed, he liked to be ready. But it looked a little silly, he knew, and he crawled out of the leather harness before climbing two flights of stairs to the tower.

The top floor was a single medium-sized room that had been turned into Ev's studio. It was well-organized, but gave the impression of untidiness because various reference photos and fashion-section clippings and preliminary drawings were taped here and there to the cream, plaster walls. The studio was filled with the expensive matching oak pieces Ev's parents had had delivered from Chicago: a pair of file cabinets, one for business papers, another (shorter, wider) for storing artwork; a bookcase stuffed with reference volumes; and a large drafting table, at which Ev sat in an office-style swivel chair, working on a large black-and-white illustration of a woman wearing a mannish pinstriped suit. She was applying watered-down india ink as a wash, making the suit gray.

She didn't notice him, at first, so lost in her work was she. Her light brunette hair was pinned up, but half-heartedly; her handsome features bore no make-up and horn-rimmed glasses hid her almond-shaped eyes. Wearing a shapeless blue smock, she was hunched over the drawing board, squinting, her right hand moving with swift, sure strokes, laying in the gray tones with a fine brush. She was sitting near the heat; his fat gray cat, Big Al, was curled up there.

"Hi, doll," he said.

She smiled immediately, but didn't take her eyes off her drawing. "What are you doing home, you big lug?"

"I told you I'd come home and spend some time before the council meeting."

"I know you did," she said, eyes still on the drawing, the smile tickling her lips. "I just didn't believe you."

"Hey, I'm an honest public servant. Everybody knows that." He looked over her shoulder. "The women are going to dress like men this year, huh?"

"Just the top layer," she said. "Still lacy underneath."

"That's a relief. Want me to go down and make us some drinks?"

"I'll go down with you," she said, and laid down a final stroke of gray. She cleaned the brush in a small glass of water on the work table next to her and grinned at him, showing perfect tiny white teeth. "There. That ought to please Mr. Bradley."

Bradley was the big boss at Higbee's department store and Ev had nothing to do with him, really; but she was always saying that.

She tossed the horn-rims on the work table, rose, stretched, showing off her nice, slender figure, pulling off the blue smock to reveal a simple white blouse and navy slacks. She was damn near as tall as he was. When she was through stretching, she slipped her arms around him and gave him a hug and then a slow, sloppy kiss.

"Don't go to that damn council meeting," she said, and pouted.

It made him laugh; she was the kind of strong woman who only pouted for effect, and when she did, it was ridiculous.

"We'll see."

"I've got a roast in the oven."

"You did believe me, when I said I'd come home."

"Hope springs eternal. Skip the council meeting."

"Why, is that what you want for your birthday?"

She grinned; she showed an expanse of pink gum when she did that—not very glamorous, he supposed, but appealing as hell.

"You remembered," she said.

He hadn't mentioned, this morning, that her birthday was why he planned to come home before the meeting.

"Let's go down downstairs, doll—you fix us some drinks. I'll start a fire."

"You already have, big boy."

He had called her "doll" almost from the beginning, which she found "corny," though she responded to it in kind.

They moved down the narrow stairway together, bumping shoulders and hips, and she went to the liquor cart and made Scotch on the rocks for him and a small pitcher of martinis for herself, while he got the fire going. He took off his tie and pitched it into the darkness; she unpinned her hair, let it tumble to her shoulders. They sat and drank and watched the glow of the fire and felt the glow of the fire and said very little, kissing frequently.

"Shouldn't we have supper?" she asked, glancing toward the kitchen.

"Dessert first," he said, nuzzling her neck.

They had dessert on the couch and after they'd got dressed again, he helped her in the kitchen. She had a mussed look that made him want dessert again, but he set the table for supper, anyway.

They ate in the kitchen. Nothing fancy. His tastes in food were simple—strictly meat and potatoes—and she catered to it. But they often ate in restaurants, particularly if she was working in the studio at Higbee's as opposed to at home. After the meal, she served him apple pie à la mode.

"Two desserts," he said, savoring a bite. "I'll get fat."

"If you want a third dessert, we can go back in front of the fireplace."

"*You* might get fat."

She smiled warmly. "I might like that."

He touched her hand. "I'd love it. I *want* children with you."

She gave him an arch look. "Are you proposing?"

They'd never really talked about it, directly.

He shrugged, smiled enigmatically, and finished his pie. Then he rose, walked to the closet by the front door and got the small package out of his topcoat pocket.

She was still finishing her slice of pie. She looked up at him, as she licked an ice-cream mustache away, and her eyes got wide as she saw the small pink-wrapped, silver-ribboned package and knew at once what it was.

She opened the little package greedily and looked at the less-than-breathtaking diamond ring as if it were more than breathtaking. She slipped the ring on and held her hand out and looked at it.

"Eliot—it's lovely! Lovely. How could you afford . . . ?"

"It's not exactly the Hope diamond, doll."

In truth, the manager of a jewelry store he'd helped out last year in the labor extortion inquiry had given him a hell of a price break.

She stood and hugged him and kissed him, a cold ice-cream kiss, but ice-cream sweet, too. He slipped his arm around her and they walked back into the living room and sat on the couch before the smoldering fire, feet up on a divan.

"Eliot . . . do we *dare* do this?"

"Sure—but we ought to keep it to ourselves."

"Like, I shouldn't wear this ring?"

"Well, not to Higbee's . . . it'd just get in the way, wouldn't it? You work with your hands, after all. . . ."

"Your reporter pals are going to know."

"They won't say anything."

"When can we . . . go public?"

"After the mayoral election. I owe that to Mayor Burton."

"That's November . . . almost a year . . ."

"I know. I'm sorry."

She sighed, but nodded; she looked at her ring wistfully. "You owe that much to Burton."

"This'll be his last mayoral campaign."

"Oh?"

"Keep it under your hat, but greater political prospects are around the corner for him."

"Governor? Senator? What?"

"Something like that."

She intertwined her legs with his. "This town'll be needing a mayor, you know."

"I suppose that's true."

"Nobody could beat you."

"Me? I'm no goddamn politician."

"Well. Nobody could beat you."

"Don't be silly."

"Think about it."

"I hate politics like poison."

"Then prove it. Skip the council meeting tonight."

"I shouldn't."

"You *owe* me, buster. You invite me to move in with you, turn this stone castle into our little love nest, and then you stay out all night all the time."

He had, in fact, been out all night several nights a week for over two months now.

He shrugged. "It's the nature of this current case."

"How do I know you're not shacking up with some floozy at the Hollenden?"

She was well aware that he had set up a second, temporary office in a suite at the Hollenden Hotel, where he was interviewing witnesses for the numbers racket investigation, often at night.

He shrugged good-naturedly. "Why don't you hire a detective to follow me?"

"What, some private eye like your friend Heller, back in Chicago? I wouldn't trust him with change for a dollar."

"Then I guess you'll just have to trust *me*."

"What the hell kind of questioning are you doing in the middle of the night?"

"Well . . . I really can't say."

"Oh for Christsake, Eliot—who am I going to tell? You trust me, and I'll trust you, okay?"

He smiled. "Okay. We have to protect the identity of our witnesses. So we pick them up in the middle of the night—if anyone's around, we pretend to be arresting 'em."

"These are all Negroes? Numbers racketeers?"

"For the most part. In some cases, we *do* arrest them, when we have somebody who we think would make a good witness, but who needs some convincing."

"What *kind* of convincing? Third-degree convincing, you mean?"

"No. That's not my style. We explain our strategy, which is to get such a large number of witnesses that no single individual can be blamed by the bad guys for any indictments that come down. We preach safety in numbers."

"So you escort these witnesses to a room in the Hollenden."

"Yes—alley entrance, up the service elevator. We spend a lot of time giving them reassurances that they'll have protection from reprisals."

"And this works?"

"We have going on fifty witnesses, at this point."

She whistled. "That's not bad—safety in numbers, all right."

There was a knock at the door. An insistent knock.

He looked over his shoulder toward the sound, suspiciously. He didn't get many people knocking at his door out here—anybody who didn't live in the subdivision would have to get by the guard at the gate, and the guard would've called ahead in such a case.

"Probably a neighbor," she said, sensing the questions he was asking himself. "Somebody needs a cup of sugar or something."

The knocking continued, obnoxiously.

"I don't think so," he said. He got up, tucked in his pants, and got a gun from the top drawer of a small desk near the front window, where he took a moment to gently part the curtains and peek out.

"It's a man," Ness said, almost whispering, "but from this angle, in the dark, can't make him out."

She was still on the couch. She said, softly but audibly, "Is that gun really necessary?"

"I hope not."

He went to the front door and stood to one side of it and called out, "Who is it?"

"Answer the goddamn door, Eliot!"

Sam Wild.

He opened the goddamn door. The cold hit him like a bucket of water. The reporter, his tan gabardine trenchcoat belted tight, his snapbrim felt hat pulled down over his eyes, hands in fur-lined leather gloves, nonetheless looked colder than hell. His breath was fog.

"Temperature dropped," Ness noted.

"Let me in, damnit! Freezing my nuts off, pardon my French."

Ness made a sweeping gesture for him to enter and Wild stepped in, shutting the door himself, then said, "Nice and toasty in here."

Ness said, sotto voce, "It's Ev's birthday, Sam. We're celebrating. This sure as hell better be important."

"It's important, all right. Your own people have been trying to call you for over an hour."

"What do you mean, trying?"

Ev's voice came from just behind him; she had snuck up on the great detective. "I'm afraid I took the phone off the hook," she admitted. "Right before dinner."

He turned and looked at her sharply.

She winced.

He sighed and worked to soften his look and, with a tense smile, said, "Please don't ever do that."

"I'm sorry," she said. She obviously meant it, but her feelings were hurt. She slipped back into the living room. He turned back to Wild.

"So?" he said, irritated.

"You ever hear of a cop named Willis? Clifford Willis?"

"No."

"He's a white cop working the Negro district. Or he was."

"Was?"

"He got shot tonight."

"Oh, Christ. Where?"

"If you're talking anatomy, he got shot a lot of places. If you're talking geography, the body turned up in the front yard of a house on Hawthorne."

"Christ! That's just a block off Central. . . ."

"Yes. A very lively colored neighborhood. And a very dead white cop. Your boys are at the scene right now. I volunteered to come fetch you."

Ness nodded. "What's the exact address?"

"5718 Hawthorne."

"Okay. Thanks, Sam. You go on. I'll be along in my own car, in a minute."

Wild nodded, said, "Sorry I busted in on your, uh, celebration."

"Don't give it a thought. See you at the scene."

Wild nodded again and went out.

Ness went into the living room, where Ev was sitting quietly, even morosely, staring at the dwindling fire.

He stood before her. "You want me to throw a few logs on before I go?"

He didn't wait for her to answer, just went ahead and did it. Got the fire going again, strong; it blazed, casting an orange glow on them.

She looked up at him yearningly. "Must you go?"

He put the iron poker back and sat down next to her. "Cop killing in the colored district."

"I understand," she said. And she did. There was nothing whiney about it; disappointment, yes—but not resentment.

He sat with her for a moment. "I didn't mean to snap at you."

"I shouldn't have taken the phone off the hook."

He said nothing.

"I just wanted to spend one damn evening with you. Is that a crime?" Here was some resentment. But no bitterness, at least.

"It's not a crime," he said. "It is a crime, leaving you alone on your birthday, though. Tell you what."

"What?"

"Make you a deal. I won't hold it against you, for the phone, if you don't hold it against me, for going."

She smiled wickedly. "Maybe I *want* you to hold it against me."

"Hold what against you? Oh. *That*. Listen, doll, I gotta go. . . ."

"This minute?"

"This minute."

He stood.

She looked beautiful, hair around her shoulders, clothes in vague disarray. "Can I wait up for you?"

"Sure. I'll try not to be long. Keep the fire going, why don't you? But if you do go up to bed, I'll wake you when I get home."

"You better."

He found his tie and put it on and the shoulder holster, too, though he left the gun behind. He was putting on his topcoat when she called to him from the living room.

"Eliot! Thank you. Thank you for the diamond."

"You're welcome, doll. Don't let the fire go out."

"I won't," she said, "if you won't."

11

Albert Curry stood looking down at the corpse, wishing it could talk.

Nervously, the cold knifing through his topcoat, he checked his watch. It was approaching nine o'clock and this slightly seedy residential neighborhood, trapped behind a wall of factories, a block north of Central off 55th, was quiet as a funeral. Quieter. Traffic was nonexistent. There were no curbside gawkers, just occasional white eyes in dark windows—not many lights on, for this time of evening. Only a few of the streetlamps were working. If it hadn't been for half a moon up in a clear, starry sky, the street would have been darker than its residents.

The paint-peeling buildings on this narrow street were for the most part your typical wide-front-porch Cleveland duplexes, run-down versions of the one he'd grown up in, and his parents still lived in, on the far east side.

On the sidewalk inside the wire fence of a small front yard filled with well-tended bushes, Toussaint Johnson stood talking to the colored couple who lived in one of the exceptions on this street: a small, neat single-family dwelling. The body had been found in their front yard, or anyway the slice of it between the front sidewalk and the wire fence. They had put frayed winter coats on over their pajamas and the man had an arm around the shoulder of his wife, who leaned into him, shivering with the cold, among other things. The husband had called in the discovery.

Curry, whose pencil and notepad were in hand, noticed that Johnson wasn't taking any field notes. That broke a fundamental rule of crime-scene technique; but Curry knew very well by now that Johnson was not a by-the-book cop. A good cop, possibly even a great cop. But not a by-the-book one.

In this instance, Curry couldn't blame him. Taking notes would only make the husband and wife ill at ease; and the benefit of having a colored cop questioning colored witnesses might well be lost.

Curry had already used ropes looped through iron stakes to fence off the corpse; he did this at the left and right, at the approximate property line, and the wire fence and the stakes with ropes made a three-sided wall. Only the street side itself was unenclosed. Using the two-way radio in his unmarked car, he had called the Detective Bureau and asked if Sergeant Merlo was on duty—which, thankfully, he was—and Merlo, who said he would call the coroner himself, should be arriving any minute now.

Curry had also called over to the Third Precinct for more uniformed men, to help preserve the crime scene, but they hadn't gotten here yet. The two uniformed cops who had got to the scene first were standing in the street; they had highway flares lit, burning orangely in the night, helping keep this deserted street deserted.

Curry and Johnson had been on the east side that evening, as usual, rounding up numbers-racket witnesses, when they heard the call come in over the police radio. They had tried to reach Ness, and had no luck; Curry stopped at a pay phone and tried the press room at City Hall, which was across from the safety director's office, figuring Sam Wild would be there. He was, but didn't know where Ness was; Wild asked Curry what the hell was going on, off-the-record, and Curry told him. Wild said he'd do his best to round Ness up, and that had been half an hour ago. No sign of either of them.

On the porch Johnson was shaking hands with the husband, and the wife was smiling a little, timidly, but smiling. They went back in their house and Johnson came down from the porch. He didn't go out the front gate. He walked over to one side of the yard, between some bushes, hopped the wire fence, and walked around on the other side of the staked-off area. He stood in the street as near as he could to Curry and the corpse without getting on the grass.

All of which went to show, Curry noted, that Johnson knew something about crime-scene preservation, when he felt like it.

"How long this joker been dead?"

"Not very," Curry said. "Jaw's still loose. No rigor yet. He's relatively warm."

"How many holes he got in him?"

"That I can see, half a dozen."

The corpse of the white man, who had been wearing a brown suit and no tie, was face-up, sprawled. The bullet wounds were in his chest and stomach—fairly small entry wounds, with scorches on the suit indicating he was shot close up.

"Wanna turn him over?" Johnson asked. "Maybe there's a weapon under him."

"We're no homicide dicks," Curry said. "Let's wait for the experts."

Johnson nodded, and Curry carefully moved away from the corpse, out into the street.

Sirens announced two squad cars of uniforms from the Third, and the spiffy new red-and-blue cars—part of the recently motorized department, Ness's highly publicized "police force on wheels"—screeched up and officers piled out like a well-organized version of the Keystone Kops. Several of them checked in with Curry and Johnson, speaking to Johnson, whom they knew, as he normally worked out of their precinct.

Curry had told them, when he radioed it in, to bring some saw-horses along, which they had, taking them from the trunks of the two squad cars and blocking off the street at either end of the block. Another round of orange-glowing flares was lit and dropped to the pavement. It seemed a pointless exercise to Curry—traffic had been nonexistent since he'd arrived—but it was procedure.

"Why's it so quiet?" Curry asked Johnson. "Usually with a homicide, you gotta beat the spectators back with a stick."

Johnson shrugged; hands in his topcoat pockets, his breath smoking. "Dead white cop in a Negro section. Wouldn't you run scared if you lived 'round here?"

"They fear reprisals, you mean?"

Johnson laughed without humor. "We two blocks from where the Joe Louis riot come down. Colored kid got shot that night."

"Oh. Yeah. That's right."

"We been working the east side together for some weeks now, Albert. You tell me. How do these people feel about cops?"

"Not good. They fear 'em. Hate 'em. Distrust 'em."

"That's right, and more. Now there's a dead ofay copper on the front lawn of a colored house. Regular east-side lawn jockey."

Curry snorted a laugh. "You could be right. We could have a riot on our hands."

"The coloreds ain't gonna riot again."

"I'm not talking about the coloreds," Curry said, and he nodded toward the white uniformed cops who were putting up the saw-horse barricades. They were talking animatedly amongst themselves, obviously angry; one of them was standing by a squad car talking into the coiled hand-mike from his police radio.

"You right," Johnson said. "That hunky's spreadin' the word. There's gonna be some black nappy skulls get crushed tonight."

"I hope you're wrong. I hope we're both wrong."

Sergeant Martin Merlo arrived with a photographer, who all but jumped out of the black unmarked sedan, left it out in the middle of the blocked-off street, and began taking pictures of the corpse and the area around the corpse. Flash bulbs popped like little gun shots, the brief explosions of light like eerie lightning.

"Looks like you've done a good job, Al," Merlo said to Curry, shaking hands ceremoniously with the younger detective. Merlo was a slender, scholarly looking man in his late forties, with horn-rim glasses and a high brow.

"Kind of tough at night," Curry said. "I haven't canvassed any of the neighbors."

"Anybody touch the body?"

"Not that we know of. Uh, do you know Detective Johnson? Toussaint, this is Sergeant Merlo."

Johnson smiled, nodded, offered his hand, which Merlo shook, smiling back professionally. "We met couple times," Johnson said. "After Kingsbury Run, Sergeant Merlo, he practically an honorary citizen of the Roarin' Third."

Merlo twitched an embarrassed smile. He had been the principal investigator of the Mad Butcher of Kingsbury Run murders, before the safety director took over the case. Though the case was considered unofficially closed, obsessive Merlo (unaware the real butcher had been secretly committed to an asylum) was still working it.

Despite Merlo's obsession with the Butcher, Curry—like his boss, Ness—considered Merlo the best homicide cop on the department. Whenever the safety director's investigators encountered a homicide, Merlo was their man.

Right now Merlo was combing the area around the dead man with a highbeam flashlight. Then he approached the body, kneeling as if to pray.

Curry, standing nearby but out in the street, said, "I checked for rigor. None yet. Body's warm. He could've been killed here."

"Doubtful," Merlo said, dousing the corpse with the flashlight; its beam landed on the face of the dead man, who had been a forty-year-old, jowly, dark-haired cop. The upper half of the man's face looked bruised.

"Somebody rough him up before they killed him?" Curry asked.

"No," Merlo said, shaking his head. "That bruising effect is lividity—when his heart stopped beating, the blood gathered on his left side, meaning he lay with his left side down when he died. Only now his left side's sunny-side up." Merlo shrugged. "They moved him."

Curry, who really hadn't worked many homicides, a little flustered at not recognizing lividity when he saw it, said, "Obviously. They dumped him here."

"But who dumped him?" Merlo said. "And why?"

Curry thought about that. He turned to Johnson. "Did you know this guy?"

Johnson yawned. "Sure. He worked the east side, out of the Third. But I don't think he was workin' tonight. And he wasn't no plainclothes."

That sparked Curry's interest. "Oh? Then what in the hell was he *doing* here?"

"Ask *him*," Johnson said, nodding toward the corpse.

Somebody was shouting over by one of the saw-horse barricades. Curry glanced over and saw Sam Wild, arguing with a uniform cop. They looked close to blows.

Curry walked over there and broke it up.

"Let him pass," Curry said.

The uniformed cop, a fiftyish paddy with a vein-shot nose, said, "On whose authority? Are you homicide?" He obviously thought Curry looked a little young to be in charge.

"I'm Detective Curry, special assistant to the safety director. Let him cross the barricade."

The older cop cleared his throat, said, "Excuse," and allowed the smirking Wild to pass.

"What's goin' on?" Wild said. "I'm anxious to see this one-man St. Valentine's Day massacre."

"You just stick with me. Don't ask anybody any questions. Did you find the chief?"

"Yeah. Big Chief Ness was makin' whoopee with his squaw. I don't think he was thrilled to be interrupted."

"So he's not coming?"

"Don't be stupid. He's damn near here."

Within moments, the EN-1 sedan was cruising past the barricade and pulled up beside Merlo's car and Ness hopped out, topcoat flapping.

"Fill me in," he said to Curry, and Curry did.

Ness went over and spoke to Merlo, who nodded as Ness gave him his orders.

Ness came over to Curry, Johnson, and Wild, and said, "We're going to keep this block cleared off. I'm having some flood lights brought in so they can comb this crime scene efficiently. So far the only physical evidence anybody's spotted is the corpse itself."

"I sure didn't see anything," Curry said. "But I think Johnson and I preserved the scene halfway decent."

"I'm sure you did. I called the Detective Bureau and they're sending half a dozen boys to canvass this neighborhood, tonight. Somebody had to have seen something."

"Don't count on it," Johnson said.

Ness considered that. "Maybe we should pull in our Negro cops and have them do the questioning."

"That would help," Johnson admitted.

Ness called Merlo over and told him to call in the request for the colored cops; any of them who were off-duty were to come in, as well.

Ness returned to the trio of men and asked Johnson, "What's your reading of this?"

Johnson's mouth twitched. He said, "Scalise did this. With Lombardi's blessin'."

"Why?"

"To cause you trouble. Dead white cop in a colored section is goin' to fire up the frictions 'tween the police and the colored citizenry."

Ness nodded gravely. "We're just a couple blocks from where that riot happened, and that kid was killed."

"Right," Johnson said. "But we also are just a few blocks

south of the white district. Easy to kill him there, dump him here.''

Wild, who was saying nothing, was lighting up a Lucky Strike; he wasn't taking notes, Curry noticed, but he wasn't missing a word.

''This does sound like Lombardi and Scalise,'' Ness said, grinning like a skull. ''We're gathering witnesses, trying to build confidence in our ability to safeguard those witnesses—and the Mayfield boys bump off a cop and dump him here. Here we are assuring witnesses of protection, and one of our own gets it, and is tossed in their literal front yard.'' He laughed bitterly.

''Hell,'' said Johnson, ''we just two and a half blocks from where one of our prime witnesses lives.''

Ness looked at him sharply. ''Who's that?''

''John C. Washington,'' Curry said. ''One of the former policy kings. You've talked to him.''

''He's a key witness, all right,'' Ness said, thinking that over. He checked his watch. ''It's not even ten. Let's go over there and talk to him. Curry, Johnson, you ride with me. Sam, you want to come?''

Wild grinned, pitched his Lucky into the night, trailing sparks. ''Sure. No more dead bodies gonna turn up here.''

As they drove the two blocks, Ness kept going over it. ''Okay, we know why they dumped the body in this district—to embarrass us, to generally . . .''

''Fuck up our investigation,'' Johnson said.

''Yes. That's exactly right. But it doesn't explain why this man . . . what was his name, Clifford Willis? Why *this* officer was killed.''

''Like we said,'' Johnson said. ''To cause trouble and embarrassment.''

''No. That's why they dumped him here. Not why they *killed* him. Johnson, you knew Willis?''

''To speak to. Worked outa the same precinct.''

''Was he Scalise's man? Was he dirty?''

''Not that I know of.''

"Jesus!" Wild said, as they rounded the corner of 46th. "What the hell is goin' on up there?"

Three red-and-blue squad cars were parked in the street at askew angles in front of the yellow frame Victorian. All the lights were on in the house, and blue shapes were moving in the windows; cops were swarming all over the front porch. There was yelling, male; there was the sound of breaking glass; there was a scream, female.

"What the hell is this?" Ness said, under his breath.

Curry glanced over at his chief, and saw the glazed, hollow look that spoke great anger on the part of this quiet man.

Ness pulled up next to the squad cars and jumped out of the sedan, leaving it running. Curry, Wild, and Johnson followed as the safety director ran up the sidewalk onto the front porch. The cops there, who seemed to be in the process of dismantling a porch swing, froze with surprise at seeing the safety director standing before them, obviously not pleased.

"What in hell are you men doing?" he demanded.

Their arms fell to their sides, swinging limply; they were like school kids caught being naughty.

He didn't wait for an answer; he moved on inside, and Curry followed. Johnson and Wild waited outside.

The inside of the house was a shambles. The beautiful little home's furniture was upended and in many cases splintered into scrap wood; the banister on the second-floor staircase had been kicked apart and its posts stuck out at odd angles, and some were gone, like a smile missing many of its teeth.

Ness wasn't smiling. This damage was being perpetrated by uniformed police officers, who were roaming the small house, trashing it, busting out windows with nightsticks, ripping drapes apart like rapists tearing the clothes off a virginal victim.

John C. Washington, dressed in silk pajamas, and his pretty, plumpish wife, who was in a silk dressing gown, were standing beside the fireplace. He had his arm around her shoulder and she was burying her face in his chest; the woman was crying, the man was standing tall, coldly furious, as his house, his possessions, were turned into rubble before his eyes, by representatives of the city government.

Ness grabbed one of the cops by the arm, a heavy-set red-haired fellow of perhaps thirty, who turned with a snarling expression, until he saw who he was snarling at, and melted like wax.

"Who's in charge?" Ness demanded, shaking him. "Who the hell's in charge!"

"No . . . nobody. We just got the call . . ."

"*What* call?"

From upstairs came the cracking of furniture getting busted up, the sound of shattering glass.

The red-haired officer gestured helplessly with both hands. "A white cop was killed, Mr. Ness. A white cop!"

"What does that have to do with *this?*"

"Johnny C. is a policy racketeer, Mr. Ness. Surely you know that."

Ness threw the man against the stairs.

He stalked back outside. Curry followed him, close as a shadow.

Ness stood in the street. Curry was at his side. Johnson and Wild were across the street on the sidewalk, just taking it all in.

"Give me your gun," Ness said to Curry.

"What are you going to do?"

"Give me your goddamn gun."

Curry swallowed. Ness swore only rarely, and hardly ever used a gun. From under his shoulder Curry withdrew the .38 revolver and handed it to Ness.

Who fired it into the air.

Once.

Twice.

Six times.

Gun still held upward, smoke twirling out the barrel, Ness stood in the middle of the street and waited.

Cops emptied out of the house like johns in a whorehouse fire. They had guns in hand and wore expressions of rage.

And they were stopped short, all of them, when they saw who was standing in the street before them.

"You men," Ness said, evenly, through teeth gritted so tight they ought to have broken, "are going to give your names and badge numbers to my assistant, Detective Curry, here. Then you're going to get the hell out of my sight. And when you're drifting off to sleep tonight, ponder this question: Why am I a police officer? And when you've searched your soul on that one, ponder this: Will I still be a police officer tomorrow morning?"

Glumly, sheepishly, they gathered around Curry, who took their names. Fifteen of them. The men muttered excuses. The word "nigger" turned up frequently, the phrase "cop killers" equally often. Within ten minutes, they were gone, their squad cars sliding slowly away, sirens off, red-and-blue tails tucked 'tween their legs.

Curry went inside, where Ness was talking to Washington and his wife. A place on a couch that was more or less intact had been cleared of rubble and glass. Washington sat with his arm around the shoulder of his trembling wife.

Ness stood before him, hat in hand. "We can put you up in a hotel, Mr. Washington."

"No, sir. I have friends in my own community."

"I can't excuse what happened tonight. But I can assure you I will have a crew from the city here tomorrow to help clean your place up. And I'll get funds to help cover the damage done."

Washington said nothing; his eyes were cold.

"There was a cop killing tonight," Ness said. "I have reason to believe your old friends Lombardi and Scalise were responsible—but they left the body on your doorstep, in effect."

Standing across the room by the fireplace, contemplating a picture in a broken frame of a fat uniformed colored soldier, Johnson said, "Cops go bughouse, Johnny, when one of their own gets it."

Washington said nothing.

Ness said, "We need your testimony, Mr. Washington. We can't let Lombardi and Scalise get away with this ruse."

Washington sighed heavily. " 'Ruse'? Does this look like a ruse to you, Mr. Ness? My home, is it a ruse? Or does it look more like a shambles?"

Curry said, "Mr. Washington—why do you think you were singled out for this?"

Nobody said anything, though Ness looked shrewdly at Curry.

Finally Washington answered: "Maybe this is going on all over the east side . . . police terrorism running rampant. There are a lot of police in Cleveland."

Ness looked at Johnson. "What do you think, Detective?"

"Johnny just happened to be close to the scene of the crime," Johnson said, matter-of-factly. "Easy target for somebody lookin' to take somethin' out on somebody."

Eyes narrowed, Ness said, "Did you know Clifford Willis? The officer shot?"

Bristling, Washington said, "Am I a suspect? We entertained friends earlier this evening, and arrived home at . . ."

Washington's wife looked at Ness with disdain.

Ness patted the air with one hand. "No . . . that's not why I'm asking. But if there's a connection . . ."

Washington stood and his wife stood with him; they might have been Siamese twins. "Mr. Ness. If you gentlemen wouldn't mind leaving me, and my wife, to what is left of our home . . . ?"

Ness nodded, sighed, stood. "We'll talk later, Mr. Washington. I'm sorry this happened."

"I should hope so."

"I don't just mean your house, Mr. Washington. A police officer was killed tonight. Let's not lose sight of that."

"Yes," Washington said, looking about his ruined home significantly. "But that's such small solace."

And the former policy king, in the midst of his stormed, sacked castle, pointed to the door.

12

Ness strode down the tunnel-like first-floor hallway of the Central Police Station like a bullet down a barrel. Cops and civilians alike got out of his way, looking downward as they did, as if feeling immediate guilt for some wrong they'd forgotten doing. He swung open the pebbled-glass door marked CHIEF OF POLICE with such force that he startled the generally sunny, blue-haired receptionist working behind the counter with several younger secretaries, all of whom looked up with similar alarm.

"The Chief back from lunch yet?" Ness said. His words were quick, clipped.

"Why, yes, Director Ness."

"Alone?"

"Yes, uh . . . would you like me to let him know you're . . . ?"

But Ness had already lifted the movable portion of the counter and moved past the receptionist, marched to the pebbled-glass marked GEORGE J. MATOWITZ, CHIEF OF POLICE and twisted the knob and pushed open the door.

He found the chief watering his precious potted plants that lined the frost-covered window just behind a vast polished mahogany desk.

"Why, Director Ness," said the chief, with a mild smile,

looking at his visitor while continuing to water a particularly flourishing plant. "This is a pleasant surprise."

"If that's what you think, George," Ness said, shutting the door firmly, taking a seat across from the desk, "then your years as chief have dulled your detective's instincts."

Matowitz frowned, not with displeasure, but confusion; he set the watering can on its designated perch on the window ledge beside the plants, and took a seat behind a desk that always seemed to Ness a little too tidy, a little too absent of any indication of real work being done.

The chief was a big, lumbering man, six feet tall and as husky as a tackle on a football squad; in his mid-fifties, Matowitz had a broad, craggy face and an amiable manner. He was relentlessly well-groomed, his dark blue uniform as crisp as a cracker, his dark blue tie neatly knotted, his badge a polished shining silver, his blue-and-white hat square on his head like that of a proud ship captain. A fresh red carnation rode his lapel; the chief did love his flowers. But his light blue eyes behind bifocal wire-framed glasses often seemed remote, to Ness, distant.

Matowitz had been a Cleveland cop since 1905. He had been chief since 1931. As a cop, he'd had a distinguished career, with two dangerous extradition cases—one to Mexico, another to Sicily—that were legendary on the force. Along the way, the determined, largely self-educated Czech-American had taken night school until he earned a law degree. But as a chief he had been too often a caretaker, content to enjoy the high position he'd worked so hard and so long to attain, enjoying his prestige, ignoring police corruption, looking forward to his pension.

When Ness came on as safety director in 1935 with a plan to clean the crooked cops out of the department, Matowitz had been told to shape up or ship out. And the plump chief had done much better since then—he'd been a loyal player on the Ness team, at least, if not the leader the chief of police really ought to be.

"Eliot," Matowitz said, humbly. "Have I done something to displease you?"

Those remote blue eyes behind the wire-frames seemed genuinely hurt; that was an encouraging sign, as was the chief's use of Ness's first name—a liberty Ness had encouraged Matowitz to take (in private), but one that the chief had rarely taken.

"We had a goddamn police riot on the east side last night," Ness said. "Or hadn't you heard?"

The eyes went remote again. Matowitz folded his hands; slowly, ever so slowly, he began to twiddle his thumbs.

"I'm aware there were difficulties last night," he said. Now his eyes became uncharacteristically hard, his jaw firm, though his thumbs continued to twiddle. "I'm also aware that one of my boys was slain."

"An officer was murdered. His body was dumped in a quiet, peaceful residential neighborhood."

"Near the Bucket of Blood."

"Near it. Not in it. I have reason to believe that white gangsters, not black ones, did the killing."

The thumbs stilled. Matowitz placed his hands palms-down on the desk. "The Mayfield Road gang?"

"Yes."

"Then this has something to do with the numbers-racket inquiry."

"It has everything to do with it. Lombardi and Scalise are trying to foul up the works."

"I see."

"No, I don't think you do. The home of one of my principal witnesses was damn near demolished last night, by fifteen of your 'boys.' They've left me with a hell of salvage job to pull off."

"Salvage job?"

"I'm going to have to dig deep in the safety department's slush fund to repay that citizen, one John C. Washington, for the damages done. If I fund his repair work, maybe I can repay what those cops did to *my* house. Maybe I'll still have a witness—although when the word spreads, I don't know why anybody else on the east side would want to volunteer for that duty."

Matowitz's features clenched like a fist. "Damnit, Eliot—a brother officer was slain! You have to expect . . ."

Ness waved that off. "I know all about losing a brother officer. I had one of my best men, my best friends, die in my arms, back in Chicago. That didn't give me a license for taking mindless revenge—and I didn't. I stayed a police officer. I did my damn job—and put the bastards who did it away."

"I think you're blowing this all out of proportion . . . one minor incident . . ."

"It was not one minor incident. I am told into the wee hours of the morning, last night, our patrolmen and detectives were prowling the Negro district, searching private citizens in bars and restaurants and private residences. Without warrants, without anything resembling due process. Systematic beatings and harassment."

Matowitz avoided Ness's glare. The chief cleared his throat and got up from his desk; he moved slowly to the bird cage in the corner where he began to feed his parakeet, whose chirping had summoned him.

With his back to Ness, he said, "I think you know how important the early hours of a homicide investigation are."

Ness turned the chair and watched the chief feed his bird. *God help me,* he thought.

He said, "Chief—did you authorize those raids?"

"I didn't authorize the raid on Washington's home."

"The others? The all-night terrorizing of the colored community by white cops? Was that your idea?"

"Not my idea, no." He smiled at the parakeet. Waggled a finger at it. Then he lumbered back to his desk and sat again. "I had an emergency call, at home, from the captain at the Third Precinct."

"Wanting to roust the populace. That is, the colored populace."

Matowitz lifted and lowered his shoulders, matter of factly. "Yes. Those searches were made with my full consent and knowledge." The chief's eyes narrowed and he raised his voice to its booming commencement-speech timbre, wagging a finger at Ness now, rather than at the bird: "No law-abiding citizen need fear a search by the police."

"Oh, horseshit, George."

Matowitz flinched at that; Ness swore so infrequently that when he did, it got a reaction. Which was when and why he did it.

Matowitz shook his head side to side. "I was backing up a homicide investigation. . . ."

"Did you receive a request from Sergeant Merlo, asking that those raids be made?"

"Well, uh—no. I did not."

"It's Sergeant Merlo's case, Chief. You don't back up a homicide investigation without checking with the detective in charge, first. Not on *my* police force you don't."

Matowitz swallowed at the reminder that the force was not the chief's, but the safety director's.

The big man sighed, as if he bore the weight of the world, and not just two hundred and twenty-seven pounds. "What do you want me to do?"

"I want you to issue a departmental directive that only officers directly assigned to the Willis investigation are to conduct raids and searches relating to that investigation."

Matowitz shook his head again. "Frankly, that seems foolish to me. The officers of the Third Precinct have a right to do something about their brother officer's death, and a responsibility to keep their eyes open on their beat, which happens to be the east side."

Now it was Ness's turn to waggle a finger. "Keep their eyes open, yes. Nothing else. This morning, I had a blistering phone call from Councilman Raney. He was outraged about these police riots, and he wants them ended *now*. And Reverend Hollis of the Future Outlook League, an influential race leader as I'm sure you know, was waiting on my doorstep when I got to the office this morning. He expressed *his* outrage, in no uncertain terms. And, last but not least, I had a friendly little call from his honor the mayor, who is anxious to maintain his own uneasy coalition with these and other race leaders. They backed him in the state election, last November, you may recall, and he wants to keep them on his side in the coming city elections."

A faint, bitter smile settled on Matowitz's lumpy face. "I didn't know you catered to politicians and lobbyists."

Ness was cold as he answered: "I cater to citizens, and I cater to the best interests of the city of Cleveland. I have an important alliance with both Raney and Hollis, an *uneasy* alliance, but an important one, without which my numbers-racket investigation would collapse like the self-control of the Third Precinct's finest last night."

Ness stood. He gave Matowitz a cold hard look. "Don't screw it up for me, George. Put the word out, officially and unofficially. Anybody who makes a mess in the Negro district is going to find his head on my plate. Like they say on Murray Hill—*capeesh?*"

Matowitz nodded. "Understood," he said.

Ness breathed air out heavily. "Good. Thank you, Chief."

Ness turned toward the door, moving past the bird cage with its well-fed parakeet; but Matowitz spoke again.

"Eliot—why this partiality to the coloreds? I know this numbers investigation is important . . . but a cop was killed, a white cop. Doesn't that mean anything to you?"

Ness turned and looked at Matowitz, noting the man's genuine confusion, and said, not unkindly, "If I'm partial to them, it's a selfish interest. I need their help and I need their trust to make my Grand Jury case float. But they're citizens, too, George."

"I didn't say they weren't, but . . ."

"No buts. I come from immigrant stock, and so do you—hell, you *are* an immigrant. If a Slovak like you can't put yourself in their place, who can?"

Matowitz grimaced with momentary embarrassment. He

nodded and looked rather blankly into space and said, hollowly, "You're right. I've always prided myself on impartially serving this town's polyglot population."

Ness recognized the phrase from speeches Matowitz had made.

The chief continued: "I've *tried* to make a sincere effort to see that . . . that everybody in this town is equal under the law."

"I know you have, George. A cop killing brings out the worst in cops. But we have to rise above it."

Ness walked over and offered his hand to Matowitz, who stood and shook it. The two men exchanged chagrined smiles, and the chief said, "I'll get that directive out right away."

"Good."

Ness was smiling when he exited the chief's office, which seemed to startle the blue-haired receptionist even more than his angry entrance; the secretaries behind the counter were buzzing amongst themselves as he went out.

In the tunnel-like corridor he was heading for the Payne Avenue exit when he heard a familiar voice call, "Hey! I been looking for you!"

He turned and smiled easily as Sam Wild, trenchcoat flying, came running up, feet echoing off the slate floor. The reporter's felt hat was in his hand. He fell in stride with Ness as they walked toward the exit.

"What flavor's Matowitz today?" Wild said, with a grin.

"What do you mean?"

"You been chewin' his ass out, haven't you?"

Ness laughed shortly. "Any answer to that question would definitely be not for publication."

"Don't bother answering. You got a car? I don't."

"Ride along, then. Why were you looking for me?"

"I got an appointment with a possible news source. I think you oughta meet him."

They stepped outside into the cold, blowing afternoon. A light snowfall was dusting the world.

"Why is that?" Ness asked, as they walked to the parking lot adjacent the four-story gray sandstone fortress that was the Central Police Station.

" 'Cause I don't think you've got a line yet, on why that cop was killed last night."

Ness said nothing. They walked up the cement ramp to the parking lot. The snow made the cement slick and they slid a bit.

Wild said, "Has that guy Johnson given any reason why he thinks Willis was shot?"

"No," Ness admitted.

"What about Sergeant Moeller?"

"No."

"Well, hell, they oughta know the straight dope on Willis. That colored cop works the same precinct, and Moeller works vice, which means he oughta know the Negro district like the back of his hand."

Ness thought for a moment before answering. "Still off the record?"

"Yeah, yeah. God help me you should actually give me any information."

"Moeller said that he heard Willis was dirty."

"Oh. Any details? Any mention of Lombardi and Scalise?"

They had stopped beside Ness's black sedan. "No. Just rumors. Let me ask you something. Why wasn't that police riot in the paper this morning, under a big Sam Wild byline? Why didn't *anybody* cover it? No radio or anything."

Wild smirked. "I'm sure the *Call and Post* will play it up big, but they're a weekly." He lit up a Lucky, cupping his hands against the snow-speckled wind. "Hell, Eliot—no paper'll touch colored news in this town. Nobody cares."

Ness felt a chill, and it had nothing to do with the weather. "What the hell are you covering this case for, then?"

The reporter blew out some smoke; where the smoke stopped and his breath began was a mystery. "The numbers investigation is different. That's a nice juicy crime story with your popular mug right in the middle of it. *That,* my friend, will get the usual headlines, black-face players or not."

Ness glowered. "A white cop was killed. What about that?"

Wild raised an unconcerned eyebrow. "It got some play."

"For a cop killing, minor. Nothing big enough for a byline. And no mention of any Negro connection, other than the address itself."

Wild shrugged, then scowled. "Hey, I'm freezing my nuts off. Let's blow."

Ness looked at him carefully. "You *did* write a story, didn't you?"

"Yeah, yeah, I wrote a story. My managing editor killed it. I knew he would, but hell—I thought if I wrote it up snazzy, and mentioned your name a couple times, I'd get my Pulitzer."

"You do care."

"Huh?"

"About the people on that side of town."

"Oh, yeah. I'm a regular missionary. Can we go?"

They got into the EN-1 sedan.

"Got a heater in this thing?" Wild said, rubbing his hands together, cigarette bobbing up and down in his mouth like a thermometer in the mouth of an impatient child.

"Yeah," Ness said, starting the car. The heat came on immediately; it was still warmed up from driving over.

Wild sighed contentedly. "God bless the taxpayers. They think of everything."

"Why don't you invest in some gloves?"

"I already did. I gave 'em away."

"Gave 'em away?"

Ness pulled out onto Payne.

"Yeah," Wild said. "To a colored guy last night."

Ness looked at him sharply. "What colored guy?"

Wild shrugged, grinned. "The one who was gonna find some stuff out for me, by this afternoon. The one we're gonna go talk to right now."

13

Karamu Theater was part of Playhouse Settlement, three old adjacent 38th Street buildings near Central Avenue that had been remodeled, over the period of years since 1915, into a recreation and cultural center for the Negro community. Two white social workers from Chicago, Russell and Rowena Jelliffe, had originally intended the settlement house to be a bridge between the white and colored populations of Cleveland; but integrated projects, like productions of biracial plays, fell by the wayside as the Roaring Third became more and more a black ghetto.

Sam Wild had done a few feature articles on Karamu Theater over the years, most recently one about the nationally prominent Negro playwright Langston Hughes, who was based in Cleveland these days and had helped mount several productions of his own works at Karamu with their resident Gilpin Players. Wild knew these occasional articles did not reflect any sense of responsibility on the part of his paper to acknowledge the existence of Negroes in Cleveland; but were rather a sop to the prominent white liberals whose financial backing made the settlement possible.

The nearby Grant Park playground was absent of children on this winter afternoon, its swing sets and slides and such powdered white by the light snowfall. A colored man wearing several heavy frayed sweaters and an equally frayed stocking cap and worn cotton gloves was sweeping the snow away from the wide walk in front of the three old but refurbished brick buildings. Sam Wild led Eliot Ness into one of them, the Karamu Theater itself.

As they angled down the aisle, the two men took in the African-themed theater (*Karamu* was, after all, Swahili for "a place of joyful meeting"). Burlap painted with striking, primitive designs hung on the walls, where the house lights were also mounted, set inside carved wooden fixtures resembling West African chopping bowls. On the ceiling shone a bright yellow sun with black rays emanating in all directions, while the proscenium had bold diagonal stripes painted on it. On the bare stage, colored actors and actresses in street clothes with scripts in hand were running through something; their voices boomed in the theater, resonant, well-articulated. Not your usual Roaring Third dialect.

Sitting about halfway down the aisle at the left was a handsome, well-groomed, chocolate-complexioned, mustached young Negro. He wore tan pants and a white shirt open at the neck. He had his feet up on the seat before him and was watching the rehearsal; he had a pad and pencil in his lap, on top of his prayerfully folded hands.

"How you doin', Katzi?"

"Samuel," Katzi said, smiling; it was a seductive smile. The man's eyes were dark and alert, amused and sad. He hauled his feet down off the seat in front of him and stepped out in the aisle. He was of medium size, five-nine and slender.

"This would be the director of public safety," Katzi said, in a tone that mixed respect with irony.

"It would," Ness said, and returned the ironic smile, and extended his hand.

Katzi shook it.

"Why don't you gentlemen have a seat here in my office?" Katzi said, with a magnanimous gesture. "If we keep our voices down, we can talk." He glanced back up at the stage.

"They're rehearsing *Porgy*—the DuBose Heyward play, not that jive-ass musical."

"Fine," Ness said, and nodded back up the aisle. "But let's sit back a ways, so we don't disturb them."

"Suits me," Katzi said, and moved up the aisle. He was as graceful as a dancer.

Wild had filled Ness in on Katzi's background, coming over. Katzi was a former policy runner and gambler who had worked for such diverse Roaring Third racketeers as "Bunch Boy" Smith, "Hotstuff" Johnson, and Johnny Perry; he had also been in solid with policy kings John C. Washington, Willie "the Emperor" Rushing, and Rufus Murphy.

Originally he had hung around with a strongarm artist named Ramsey, and the pair had been nicknamed "Big Katzi" and "Little Katzi" after the Katzenjammer Kids in the funnies. But Ramsey wasn't around anymore, and now Little Katzi was just plain Katzi.

Katzi, who'd had some college, had at one time possessed a reputation for violence. "Little Katzi will kill you," had been the word, from the pimps, hustlers, gamblers, and whores of the Roaring Third. He had packed a .44 Colt revolver and had once pistol-whipped the white proprietor of a restaurant on the fringe of the ghetto when refused service. A few years back, Katzi had done a stretch at the Ohio pen for armed robbery. He was on parole now.

Wild had only known Katzi for the past two years; but he liked and respected, warily, the charming if unpredictable young Negro. In the pen, Katzi hadn't been required to do hard labor, having a disability pension from the Ohio State Industrial Commission for a work injury years before. Instead he'd spent his time teaching himself to be a writer, and began publishing articles and stories in Negro weeklies like the *Call and Post* and then in pulp magazines like *Abbott's* and finally (making Wild somewhat envious) selling short stories to *Esquire* and *Coronet*.

Katzi was the only colored reporter in Cleveland; true, he was basically just a stringer, writing vignettes for the editorial pages of the *News*. But it was a singular distinction nonetheless, and he was currently working on the WPA writers project, writing the history of Cleveland for the Ohio guidebook.

Ness edged into the final row of seats at the rear of the theater; Katzi followed and Wild followed him. The three men sat and Wild asked Katzi if it was okay to smoke in here.

"It is if you offer me one," Katzi said, and Wild did.

Wild lit Katzi's Lucky, and asked, "How's the WPA writing comin'?"

"Beats diggin' sewers for 'em," he said. "Last year this time, I was dredging creeks in the snow and ice, out in the suburbs. As WPA gigs go, this one's a plum."

"You going to write a paragraph on Karamu in the guidebook?"

"Naw. I'm doin' a little piece on it for Howard."

N. R. Howard was the editor of the *News*.

Wild lit his own Lucky. "How's the prison novel comin'?"

"Done. Showin' it around, without much luck. So, Samuel. Is that why you wanted to get together? To ask me about my career? Oh, hey, thanks for the gloves, man. I'm makin' a livin' writing, but just barely. A buck a piece for these damn 'vignettes' don't go very far."

Wild reached in his coat pocket and withdrew a ten-dollar bill. "How far will this go?"

Katzi grinned, his eyes flickered. "The meter is runnin'."

Ness said, "Was Clifford Willis a dirty cop?"

Katzi shifted in his seat and grinned lazily at the safety director. "That depends on how you define dirty."

"Why don't you define it for me, then."

"In your way of thinking, Willis was dirty. Where I come from, the numbers is a part of the way things are, and so is paying off a cop for protection. But, yeah. He was on the pad, to the numbers racketeers."

"Scalise and Lombardi, you mean."

Katzi blew out smoke; up on the stage the actors were emoting, their voices echoing like an insistent conscience.

"That's recent history," Katzi said, with an easy smile.

"Go back a few years, when the Emperor opened his first policy house. Before that, Rufus Murphy had the only policy house in Cleveland, the Green House. He made sweet money, Rufus did—that illiterate son-of-a-bitch sent his daughter to school in Paris."

Ness was listening politely, but Wild could tell he wanted Katzi to get to the heart of things.

But Katzi was a storyteller and couldn't be hurried. "So Emperor Rushing, who was running gambling houses up till then, sent for a pal in Chicago name of Cateye, who knew the policy racket, and they opened up the Tijuana House. After the Emperor opened his house and was real successful, a lot of colored hustlers, gamblers, pimps, club owners, businessmen got in on the act and opened houses of their own. The policy racket was booming."

"Which means," Ness said, "the cops working the Negro district went on the take."

"It sure does. And Willis was working that beat as a patrolman."

Ness sighed. "What about Toussaint Johnson?"

"What about him?"

"Was he on the pad?"

Katzi's eyes narrowed shrewdly. "I understand Toussaint is workin' with you these days."

"That's right."

"So do you really want to know the answer to that question?"

Ness said nothing. Then he nodded.

"Well," Katzi said, with a big grin, "I don't think I'll answer it, anyway. Toussaint is a hell of a guy—and I can tell you this, he is not on the pad, today. He hates those Italian mobsters like fire hates water. He is not on the pad. You dig? You understand?"

"Yes," Ness said.

"But Willis was," Wild said. "On the pad."

Katzi nodded emphatically. "When policy was booming,

and the alky mob got Repeal dropped in their ugly laps, that's when Black Sam and Little Angelo muscled in."

"Did you witness any of that?" Ness asked, quickly.

"No. I was in the pen at the time. When I went inside, Rufus, the Emperor, and Johnny C. were on top of the world. When I come out a couple years ago, they were dead, turned stooge, and retired, respectively. And Willis was on the Scalise and Lombardi payroll."

"I see."

Katzi laughed; it was mellow. "You know, you were the best thing that ever happened to Willis."

"Me?" Ness said, shocked.

"Willis was a patrolman, remember. He had a taste of the take, but nothin' major, mind you. When you come in back in '35 like a big brass band, you shook things up by transferring cops from one precinct to another, all over town."

"Right," said Ness, somewhat defensively. "That upset crooked apple carts all over the city."

"Sure it did. It was smart. Hey, I'm not bein' critical, Mr. Ness. And a whole lot of those transfers you made were big cheeses. Officers—captains and lieutenants and sergeants and detectives. Am I right?"

"Of course you are," Ness said, trying to mask his confusion, not terribly well. "That's where the power was. We had a crooked department within the real department, in those days. They had their own structure, their own 'chief.' "

"I know. You sent a whole bunch of those high-ranking boys to the pen, including their chief. Hell—I *met* some of 'em there, and you'll be glad to know it was no picnic for 'em."

Now Ness smiled. "I'm not sorry to hear that, no." The smile faded. "But you still haven't said exactly how it is I'm 'the best thing that ever happened' to the late patrolman Willis."

"You transferred all the big boys outa the Roarin' Third," Katzi said, with a matter-of-fact shrug. "Who did you think was gonna move up into position? A patrolman like Willis, who was on the pad already, and still working the Roaring Third! The new higher-ranking boys were afraid to take a piece of that action, with you in town, throwing crooked captains and the like in the clink."

Ness was nodding. "So Willis, a relatively little fish, fell through the cracks of the system. And became a bigger fish because he was in the right place at the right time."

"That's the story, Mr. Ness. And you know, a crook has no morals. He'll work for anybody, if they got the dough."

"What are you saying?"

Katzi blew out blue smoke, shrugged, smiled one-sidely. "The reason why Willis was killed was he went against Lombardi and Scalise."

"In what way?"

"You know that killing over at the Elite Cabaret, a while back?"

"Of course."

"Well, what do you know about it, exactly?"

Ness seemed on the verge of irritation; he didn't like a snitch who asked questions. "We know that it represents the Mayfield Road gang chasing that Pittsburgh bunch out of the city. Scaring them off Lombardi and Scalise's turf. And we suspect Scalise himself murdered those men."

"That's the word on the street on the subject," Katzi confirmed. "But can you prove it?"

"We traced a bloody coat from the alley of the Elite to a haberdashery where Scalise has done business—but we couldn't find a clerk to admit making the sale, or a sales slip either."

"Five'll get you ten," Katzi said, "Scalise killed Willis, too. Personally."

"What makes you say that?"

Katzi shrugged again. "Scalise is meaner than a drunk snake. He likes hurtin' people. He likes killin' people. Everybody in the Roaring Third knows that."

Ness had an intense expression. "And why would he've killed Willis, his own man, a cop he had in his own pocket?"

"That's what I been telling you, Mr. Ness. Few months back, Willis did business with the Pittsburgh boys."

Ness looked sharply at Wild; there was the motive. At last. There was the motive.

"Word on the street," Katzi was saying, "is that the Pittsburgh outfit offered Willis more than Scalise and Lombardi were payin', if he'd help 'em move in. And he did. And he dead."

Ness digested that, then asked, "Why'd they wait so long to pay Willis back for his betrayal?"

"How should I know? Maybe to keep you from putting two and two together. Maybe to make Willis sweat some before they chilled him. Maybe to line up a new cop fixer, first. Hell, you're the detective."

Ness thought about that.

Katzi crushed his cigarette under his heel on the theater floor. "Think you can put those mother-raping dago bastards away, Mr. Ness?"

"Oh yes," Ness said.

"Good. I got no love for 'em, myself."

"Why's that?" Wild asked. Katzi didn't seem to him the sort of guy who would give a damn one way or the other.

"Oh, they killed my cousin a few years ago," he said, casually. "One of the independent policy operators they rubbed out."

"What was his name?" Ness asked.

"Willie Wiggens," Katzi said, emotionlessly.

Ness looked at Katzi long and hard.

Then he said, "Thank you, Katzi," and shook the man's hand again. Any irritation had vanished; bare gratitude had taken its place. He dug into his topcoat pocket. "Here's a little more for you."

He handed Katzi a fin and the smoothly affable Negro took it gladly.

"If there's anything else I can do for you," Ness said, "let me know. Information like this is greatly appreciated."

"Well, you can put a word in for me with the parole

board," Katzi said, as they all stood, and moved out into the aisle. "I'd like to get my citizenship restored and put the past behind me."

"That's an admirable goal," Ness said. "I'll see what I can do."

"Appreciate it. But I got no delusions about the past going away altogether."

"I know what you mean," Ness said, with a glum smile. The past had, after all, caught up with him today.

Wild nodded and smiled to Katzi, who said, "See you in the funny papers, Samuel," and sauntered down the aisle and took a closer seat, watching the rehearsal, where deep voices boomed.

Out in the gently blowing snow, the wind nipping at them, Wild said to Ness, "How's that for a source?"

"Goddamn good," Ness admitted. "But it frustrates me that I had to come here to get it."

"Hey, come on. Using stoolies is what police work is all about."

"Maybe. But I hate like hell to have to get from a stoolie information that my own men are keeping from me."

On the way back, Ness looked over, from behind the wheel of his sedan, and said, "Is that fellow a good writer?"

"Better than I am," Wild said with a smirk.

"I ought to read something of his. What's his real name?"

"Himes," Wild said. "Chester Himes."

"I'll try to remember that," Ness said.

"Remember him to the parole board," Wild said, "if you're really interested."

Ness nodded.

But Wild could see that the safety director was already lost in other thoughts. Thoughts of Lombardi and Scalise, and a police department that even after all of Ness's efforts and successes in cleaning it up remained a fortress of self-interest.

· THREE ·

APRIL 25–MAY 1, 1939

14

Ness was behind the wheel of a black unmarked Ford sedan—but not the one with the familiar-around-town EN-1 license plate: No calling card was required or desired on this excursion.

It was shortly after midnight on a pleasantly cool Tuesday in April; the moon was a shining silver-white plate that reflected on the hood of the sedan as Ness eased into a parking space just down the street from his destination. Jammed in the car with him were two plainclothes men and two uniformed. He checked his watch.

Two minutes.

The apartment building was just north of Case Western Reserve, overlooking the vast garden that was Rockefeller Park, on Ansel Avenue. A five-story graystone with terra cotta trim, the building had a uniformed doorman and, one would think, well-to-do or anyway well-off tenants.

One of those tenants was Willie "the Emperor" Rushing, one-time policy king, current front man for the Mayfield Road gang. Undoubtedly one of the few Negro residents of this obviously predominantly white neighborhood.

Ness was leading one of five squads that were about to simultaneously attack key numbers-racket figures. Two months ago he had delivered to Prosecutor Cullitan a document as thick as a popular novel; that document detailed the evidence and gathered the statements of seventy witnesses against twenty-three members of the Mayfield Road mob—including Salvatore Lombardi and Angelo Scalise.

After interviewing the witnesses himself, Cullitan had gone forward. For the last two weeks, those seventy witnesses paraded secretly through the Grand Jury room, with no press coverage and no apparent leaks to the mob; and tomorrow the indictments were to come down, naming all twenty-three defendants.

It was going so well it made Ness uneasy.

"We're taking no chances," Ness had told the startled group of detectives who without advance warning had been summoned (from home, in many instances) to the safety director's office at City Hall, for an eleven P.M. meeting. "We're not giving these bastards any opportunity to take a powder."

Pointing at a wall map of Greater Cleveland, with appropriate pins stuck in twenty-three positions, he explained that there would be five unmarked cars with twenty-five men divided between them. Around the table sat Moeller, Curry, Chamberlin, Garner, and Toussaint Johnson.

"It'll be a mass round-up," Ness said, with a tight smile. "We'll hit the first five targets at the precise same moment—synchronizing by police radio. Five minutes after each raid goes down, a paddy wagon will roll up in front and you'll load 'er up with bad guys."

"Sounds simple," Garner said, wetting the end of a fresh fat cheap cigar. "Any special charge? Never heard of arresting crooks the day before indictments were voted."

"Jail them as suspicious characters and hold them for investigation," Ness said. "That's good enough for Prosecutor Cullitan, and it's good enough for me."

One team would hit the Central-Scovill district; that would be led by Moeller with Curry and Johnson lending support. Two teams, led by Chamberlin and Garner respectively, would head for Cleveland Heights, where (among others) Lombardi himself lived. Detectives Powers and Allen, who had already been dispatched, would hit the far northeast side of Cleveland. Ness himself would hit three targets, two of them clustered together at East 90th and East 93rd, and another just north of that on Ansel.

It frustrated Ness that he couldn't be in on the collar of Lombardi and Scalise, personally; but realistically, as the leader of this mass offensive, Ness could not head up one of the outlying teams. He needed to be able to round up his quota of suspects quickly, and get to Central Station to supervise the booking and questioning of everybody else's prisoners, as well as his own, as they were hauled in.

But when Chamberlin paused while lighting up his pipe to ask the safety director why he wasn't claiming the Lombardi/Scalise collar for himself, Ness offered a different excuse.

"I'm an old Chicago boy," Ness said, smiling a little. "To me Cleveland Heights is all hills and winding roads. Even with a driver, I'd feel lost. You'll do a better job, Bob."

Albert Curry seemed stuck somewhere between confused and annoyed as he said, "Why are you putting Moeller and Johnson and me on the same team?"

"Two reasons," Ness said. "You're hitting the heart of the ghetto—it's going to be unpredictable and precarious down there. Obviously, Detective Johnson will be a great asset in that neighborhood, and Sergeant Moeller is an old hand at raids of this sort."

"This won't be my first raid, either," Curry said, obviously a bit offended that he wasn't heading up one of the teams himself. "And you said *two* reasons . . ."

Ness looked at Moeller and said, "Care to explain, Sergeant?"

Moeller, who was sitting next to Curry, offered a twitch of an apologetic smile and said, "I had a call this afternoon, from somebody in Hollis's camp . . . one of these Future Outlook League members. Seems there's a men-only party tonight at League Hall. Six of our suspects are gonna be there."

"What's League Hall?" Curry asked.

"State Democratic League," Johnson put in. "The Negro Democrats' HQ. Eighteenth Ward Junior Democratic Club is puttin' on this smoker tonight . . . there will major policy guys on hand."

"This sounds political," Curry said. "Hollis is a Republican—maybe he just wants to embarrass the opposition."

"That may be the motivation behind the tip," Ness said, "but *we* won't play it for politics." He lifted a forefinger. "No arrests other than the policy guys. Understood? I don't want any reporters tagging along with you."

"Press been tipped?" Garner asked.

"Not yet," Ness said. "But on my way out, I'm going to see who's in the press room—if anybody's on the job, I'll tell 'em to head over to Central Station and wait for a story to fall in their laps."

Now, at exactly ten after midnight, Ness spoke into the hand mike on the coiled rubber cord and said, "Go."

He stepped out of the sedan. It was cool enough for a topcoat, but he hadn't worn one; his suitcoat was unbuttoned and his revolver was in its shoulder holster. He and officer Claude Lewis, a Negro patrolman who was in plainclothes tonight, walked the half-block to where the doorman stood, while one of the uniformed officers waited by the car and another of the uniformed officers went around to cover the rear of the building.

The doorman was a big pink man about forty who in his elaborate uniform with epaulets looked like a chorus member in a Victor Herbert operetta. It was a role he took seriously, however, because he held out his hand in a pompous stop gesture.

"This is a private building," he said, chin up, eyes down.

"This is public business," Ness said, pleasantly, and with a thumb lifted his lapel to reveal the gold safety director's shield.

The doorman looked down his nose at the badge and Ness grunted and brushed the big man aside, then pushed the glass door open and went in; behind him, Patrolman Lewis was telling the doorman, "Don't warn 'em upstairs, or you'll be an accessory."

The offended but now docile doorman didn't reply, although it might have been a fair question to ask accessory to what.

The lobby was small, clean, and modern, with assorted mirrors and potted plants; Ness and the patrolman took the elevator up to the third floor, where in Suite 3C the Emperor ruled his roost.

Ness knocked on the bright red door. Three hard, rifle-shot knocks.

There was no response.

He knocked again. Three more hard rifle shots.

"Guess I'll have to kick it in," Ness said, matter-of-fact but purposely loud.

A muffled female voice from behind the door called out: "Willie ain't here!"

Ness spoke to the door. "Are you Mrs. Rushing?"

There was a pause. "I is gonna be."

"Who am I speaking to?"

"Jewel LaVerne. We engaged."

"Well, that's very romantic, Miss LaVerne. Open the door, please. We have a warrant."

"Let me see it."

"Open the door, Miss LaVerne, and I'll show it to you."

She reluctantly eased open the door, halfway, leaning against the doorjamb with studied insolence that failed to mask her fear; a yellow-complexioned girl of perhaps twenty, she had a round face with sultry, long-lashed eyes and a full mouth and a lack of make-up made her no less sullenly pretty. She was wearing a man's silk pajamas, which filled out interestingly, sleeves and pant legs rolled up to accommodate her shapely five-five frame. She smelled of lilac perfume and sleep.

Ness dug the folded warrant out of his suitcoat pocket and showed it to her. She looked at it blankly; his guess was she couldn't read.

She looked at him, batting her lashes in slow motion and gazing at him like a bored cat; but there was tension in the eyes nonetheless.

"Willie ain't here, I tole you. He's outa town."

"Where, out of town?"

"Two hundred miles away."

"Please stand aside, Miss LaVerne."

The sullen face squeezed into a childish pout and she stepped back and slammed the door in Ness's face, damn near breaking his nose.

He stood back, feeling more stupid than angry, rubbed his sore nose, and sighed.

Patrolman Lewis asked, "You want me to bust it down?"

"No thanks," Ness said, with a faint smile. "This is a specialty of mine."

He kicked the red door three times, with the flat of his foot, emphasis on the heel, enjoying the feel of the impact as it climbed the muscles of his leg, shaking his whole body, rattling his teeth. The door sprang open on the fourth kick and Ness knifed through the apartment, pushing the sweet-smelling woman aside. The apartment was ornately furnished, the carpets thick-napped Orientals; the Emperor had himself a palace, all right.

"Stay out here," Ness ordered Lewis. "Keep an eye on her, and the door!"

Ness quickly found the bedroom, a room so garish it startled him, from the fancy brocade wallpaper, blood-red, to the ornate white furniture and huge polished brass bed with red silk sheets and overhead mirror. The smell of the woman's lilac perfume was in the room.

Willie was, too.

The big middle-aged man was climbing out the window—while his girl had been stalling the cops, fastidious Willie had taken time to get dressed, in a powder-blue shantung-silk suit and pale yellow crepe linen-silk shirt with a dark blue silk-knit tie. He was weighted down with gold jewelry—

rings and cufflinks and diamond stickpin—and in his left hand was an alligator traveling bag.

"All dressed up and nowhere to go, Willie," Ness said, standing with his hands on hips, grinning. "Except jail, of course."

Willie stepped back inside; he let the alligator bag drop to the floor and put his jewelry-heavy hands up and his smile was as wide and white as a picket fence.

"Mister Ness," he said. "I was jus' about to leave town on business."

"Were you," Ness said, approaching Willie cautiously. "Do I have to cuff you, Willie, or will you come along quietly?"

"What the charge?"

"We're just going to hold you for questioning. No big deal."

"Fine with me, boss," Willie said, and he shoved Ness with two big hard hands, knocking him back against the foot of the brass bed. Willie slipped out the window, with a deep laugh, and Ness picked himself up and smiled tightly and went after him, catching him on the fire-escape landing.

Willie turned and swung a ham-size fist, but Ness ducked it, tackling Willie; the two men slammed into the metal railing and began wrestling, and soon the Emperor, a big bear of a man, was on top, the cross-hatching of the metal grillwork digging into Ness's back. The cool night was damn near day, with the full moon above, and Ness could see clearly the vicious expression over him as the Emperor drew back a massive fist and was about to let fly, when Ness grabbed the gun out from under his shoulder and pointed it straight up into the big man's face.

The Emperor's two white wide eyes looked down into the smaller black infinite one of the .38 and he froze, his drawn-back arm and fist caught in midair, as if stiffened there.

"Think about it, Willie," Ness said. "You can be dead, or we can go back inside and pretend this never happened."

The Emperor swallowed and smiled the picket-fence grin

again and crawled off Ness like a satisfied lover. He stood on the fire-escape landing and brushed off his fancy silk suit with whisk-broom hands.

"Pretend *what* happened, Mr. Ness?" Willie asked innocently.

Ness was on his feet now. It was a little windy up here, he noticed.

"Are you all right, Mr. Ness?" the patrolman below called up. The fire escape was on the east side of the building and it had taken a while for the man stationed out back to notice the struggle.

"Everything's under control," Ness yelled down. Then to Willie, with a gesture of the .38, he said, "After you, Emperor."

Willie stepped back inside.

"Them indictments is comin' down," Willie said, "ain't they?"

"Let's put it this way," Ness said. "You're about to be deposed."

Ness led the man through his apartment, where the girl stuck her pink pointy tongue out at the safety director; Ness, Rushing, and Lewis went down the elevator and out front, where a Black María was waiting.

Lewis stood eagerly by as the paddy wagon officer closed the back door of the buggy on the glumly seated Emperor, and Ness checked his watch.

"We're on schedule," Ness said to Lewis, "but barely. Let's go."

15

The Demo League Hall was at East 71st and Central, a huge yellow-brick two-story building that came right up to the sidewalk in a thriving ghetto business district. The lower floor of the building was taken up by small businesses— liquor store, delicatessen, tavern, drug store. Curry stood, in the light of the moon and streetlamps, studying with a tourist's curiosity the cluttered display behind the iron-grilled window of Cohn's Drug, an array that included blood tonics, skin bleaching creams, and electric hair-straightening irons.

Finding a place to park the unmarked sedan had been a trick; both sides of the street were thick with parked cars. They left it in the alley behind the massive building, Moeller saying it wasn't a bad idea blocking the alley, anyway. The windows up on the second floor were dark and shut tight, but the sound of a raucous party going on was seeping out nonetheless.

They needed to move fast; they'd just been given the go-ahead from Ness on the police radio to make the hit, and that meant a paddy wagon would automatically arrive in five minutes, ready for a load of reluctant passengers.

The small sign that extended over the street said DEMO-CRATIC LEAGUE HALL in red letters on yellow, with a smaller black-letter notice: *Available for Rental*. Stocky vice cop Moeller—in plainclothes tonight—led the way, with Toussaint

Johnson next, and Curry bringing up the rear. One uniformed man stayed down on street level, and another was in the alley with the car.

It was a narrow, steep, dark stairwell, with the only light at the second-floor landing above. The door was unlocked, but just inside the door a cigar-smoking, beer-bottle-clutching heavy-set Negro in a white shirt and suspenders sat at a card table with an open cigar box full of dollar bills and ticket stubs.

The burly Negro in a gravelly voice asked them if they had tickets, but Curry, as he stepped into the hall, barely heard the man. He was overcome by the sights and sounds and smells confronting him. The air was blue-gray with cigarette and cigar smoke which mingled with the stink of body odor, beer, and bad breath.

The high-ceilinged, many-windowed hall was crammed with banquet-style tables at which at least three hundred men—at least a third of them white—sat applauding and hooting as down on the stage at the far end of the hall a voluptuous young yellow-skinned stripper in a G-string and tassels was doing a bump and grind to a blaring version of "St. Louis Blues" from a scratchy record that was playing through a distorted but loud sound system. Several other strippers, of various Negro shades, were wandering through the audience, specifically enticing a group near the stage who were seated not at tables but on thirty or forty folding chairs; the men were grabbing at the women, stuffing money in their G-strings, generally playing grab-ass. Occasionally a stripper would light on the lap of one and wriggle. A good number of the men up in front, Curry noted, were white.

The fat Negro ticket-taker was almost yelling, now. "I said, do you boys have tickets? If not, cash will suffice."

Toussaint Johnson edged out in front of Moeller and said, "We're the men."

"Christ," the fat man said, knowing that Johnson meant they were cops. "Is this a fuckin' raid? You're raidin' the Democratic League smoker? What the hell's the idea?"

Working to get his voice heard, Moeller said, "We have warrants on six men who we believe are present in this hall at this time."

The formality of that struck Curry as strange and even silly, as he watched two strippers scamper out of the audience up a staircase at either side of the stage and the three women began bumping and grinding in tandem. The yellow girl, who had bosoms that looked formidable even from this distance, was twirling her tassels, one in one direction, one in the other. It was the goddamnedest thing Curry had ever seen.

But he was cop enough to snap out of it and he stepped forward and touched Moeller on the arm.

"This is trouble," he whispered right into the man's ear. "We got political people here, Negro *and* white—the boss is going to have a shit fit, if this gets out of hand."

Up on the stage, the central girl, the yellow one, was plucking off her tasseled pasties and flinging them into the eager audience; they were whooping and hooting and generally behaving like cheerful but hungry lions being tossed slabs of meat. The other girls followed suit—birthday suit, that is.

"It's already out of hand," Moeller said, watching this.

Curry could read him; Moeller was a vice cop, and Curry knew what he was thinking.

"Don't do it," Curry said.

The girls were sliding out of their G-strings.

"Shit," Moeller said.

"Let it go," Curry said.

"He's right," Toussaint Johnson said. "Let's wait downstairs by the exit and nail the boys we want as they come out."

"We have two more pick-ups to make," Curry reminded them both.

"St. Louis Blues" ended and "Hold That Tiger" took over, just as scratchy, just as loud, inspiring even more frenetic gyrations from the strippers and even wilder response from their appreciative audience.

"Go on ahead and leave me behind," Johnson said. "With one of the uniforms. I'll nab 'em."

The girls were flinging their G-strings into the audience.

"I can't look the other way on this," Moeller said, shaking his head.

Curry couldn't look the other way, either, not in the literal sense anyway, but he said, "The boss just wants the policy suspects."

A very drunk white man, his tie loose around his neck, his shirt half unbuttoned and hanging out, danced up onto the stage and began fondling the bosomy yellow-skinned stripper. She laughed. Curry couldn't hear the laugh, over the hollering and distorted sound-speaker music, but he could see her laughing, and now she was starting to undo the man's pants. The crowd was going berserk.

"That's it," Moeller said, shaking his head. "This is lewd and indecent conduct. I'm hauling all their asses in. Johnson, go downstairs and call over to the Third Precinct and get every goddamn spare squad car they got over here—and every paddy wagon."

Curry said, "Don't do it!"

He wasn't sure if he was talking to Moeller or the woman on stage who seemed about to perform an act of oral sex on the inebriated but obviously capable male dance partner. Curry had heard of audience participation before, but this was ridiculous.

"And tell 'em to come with their sirens blaring," Moeller said, "so I know when they're here. We're going to shut this fucker down."

"You say so," Johnson shrugged to Moeller, and went out.

Moeller turned to the fat man on the door, still seated at his card table, and said, "Not a word out of you. Don't move a goddamn muscle."

"You got it, boss," he said unenthusiastically.

The yellow girl on stage now had hold of the man, whose trousers were gathered absurdly around his ankles, and was leading him offstage, into the wings, as if walking a dog. The man was grinning; he walked like a penguin. The naked yellow woman and the grinning white man disappeared from sight and the audience began to cheer. It struck Curry as disgusting and unreal and a little exciting; but most of all, he was dismayed that vice cop Moeller had strayed from the objective.

"When you hear police sirens," Moeller was telling the fat man, "hit the lights."

The fat man swallowed and nodded; he looked like his best friend had died.

Johnson emerged from the stairwell—he didn't look much happier than the fat man. "Be about three minutes," Johnson said.

Curry knew that was no exaggeration. Ness had worked hard to get the response time of the department's squad cars to a minimum.

Soon sirens were wailing, and the lights came up in the room and hundreds of men of several races turned faces as distorted as the music toward the back of the room in shock and even anger, and the naked strippers on stage froze momentarily, then lost their composure, the bright lights having turned them from nude to naked.

Moeller stepped forward with his badge held high in one hand. "It's a raid, gents!"

And Curry watched with amazement as dozens of the men headed for the side windows and began climbing out, jumping from the sinking ship that was the Democratic League Hall, risking the second-story drop.

Ness snapped the cuffs on the sleeping man, then nudged him awake.

"Lawrence," he said, as the slender handsome Negro sat up in bed startled, "you're under arrest."

Lawrence Gasior, who ran one of Emperor Rushing's policy houses, glanced at his pretty young wife, who sat up in bed next to him, gathering the covers around the front of her, looking at him with wide searching eyes.

His gun was in his wife's handbag way in the kitchen; might as well have been in France. His bedroom was filled with uniformed cops and the safety director of the city of Cleveland.

"Ain't this the damnedest thing," Lawrence said.

Bob Chamberlin, at the mansion-like home of Salvatore Lombardi on Larchmere in Cleveland Heights, had come up empty. Nobody was home but the servants.

He called the bad news in, just as Garner, at a fancy apartment house on Eddington just off Superior, was discovering that Angelo Scalise had flown the coop as well.

By dawn Ness was sitting in his office, with Curry, Garner, and Chamberlin; everybody else had gone home. The bad guys had been booked—of the twenty-three men on whom warrants were issued, all but six were rounded up.

So, unfortunately, had been some three hundred men who attended the smoker at the Demo League Hall. A dozen paddy wagons had shuttled the angry and embarrassed guests to the Central Station, where they were allowed to sign waivers and were released. The booking agent for the strippers, who had shown obscene films to the group earlier in the evening, was among those arrested, as were the strippers themselves, girls in their twenties who had prostitution arrests on their records.

Several dozen of the party-goers, who escaped the indignity of arrest, would be sporting wrenched backs and sprained ankles and worse, today, from jumping out the windows last night.

"Will the papers cover it?" Chamberlin asked. His pipe was in his hand, unlit.

All four of the men looked haggard, their beards heavy,

their eyes bloodshot. All but Ness had their coats off and slung over the backs of their hardwood chairs; and even Ness had his tie loosened.

"No," Ness said. "Only the *Call and Post.*"

"Why?" Curry asked. "Sam Wild and Fritchey and Kelly and Seeley were at the station when those paddy wagons rolled in."

"Colored news," Garner said with a wry smirk. He had a cigar in his mouth, but it had gone out and he wasn't bothering to light it.

"Not everybody who was arrested was colored," Curry insisted.

"Most were," Chamberlin said, with a soundless laugh. "And as for those who were white, the local press wouldn't want to embarrass any prominent Clevelanders, now, would they?"

"Was this a disaster tonight," Curry said, honestly wondering, "or a success?"

"A qualified success," Ness said, though his expression was close to a scowl. He got up slowly and moved to the big wall map and began plucking out pins. Only six remained when he was done. "We've got everybody but a few of the bigger fish—and we'll get them, too."

"Were they tipped, d'you think?" Chamberlin asked.

"How?" Curry asked. "None of us knew about these raids until we were seated in this room, just hours ago."

"I don't mean to imply anybody was tipped about tonight's round-up," Chamberlin said, gesturing with the unlit pipe. "But it was no deep secret that indictments were in the wind."

Ness sat on the edge of the table. "Bob's right. We're lucky our net pulled in as many fish as it did. And today I'll call my friends at the Justice Department and get a national sweep going."

"What if Lombardi and Scalise and the rest skipped the country?" Curry asked.

"That's tougher," Ness admitted. "But there's such a thing as extradition. We won't give up on 'em."

"Great," Curry said. "Then why don't you look happy?"

Ness sighed heavily. He hesitated for a moment, then said, "I let Hollis and Councilman Raney make a fool of me. I was stupid to think I could contain the politics of that situation over at the League Hall."

"I'll bet Hollis knew it was going to be a big, rowdy, randy scene," Chamberlin said. "That wasn't your average smoker for a dozen lodge brothers."

"No it wasn't," Ness said.

"Where's Sergeant Moeller?" Curry asked. His tone lacked respect.

"I sent him home. He seemed pretty embarrassed about the way things came down."

"He should be."

Chamberlin snorted. "Did he really have to go all moral and bust that shindig?"

Ness looked carefully at Curry, who said, indignantly, "*I* don't think he did."

"From the police report," Garner said, unlit cigar roaming his mouth, "it sounds like the kinda party Nero mighta fiddled at."

"Well," Curry admitted, "yes, it was, kind of."

"Under normal circumstances," Ness asked, "would you have busted that party, Albert?"

"Well . . . well. Yes, I suppose I would've. Under normal circumstances."

"You suppose?"

Curry breathed out his nose like a bull considering goring a matador. "I would've."

Ness shrugged. "Moeller was just doing his job. Making a decision under fire, as we all must, from time to time. I'm going to stand behind him on it . . . without being thrilled over the results."

"Johnson isn't here, either," Garner noted.

"I sent him home, as well," Ness said. "Albert—did you

think Johnson knew what you were in for, at that smoker?"

"No. Not really."

"You don't think he was working for the interests of Hollis and Raney?"

"No," Curry said, shaking his head emphatically. "He felt as uneasy as I did, about raiding the place."

Ness said nothing, thinking.

"Where do we go from here?" Chamberlin asked.

The sun was sneaking in around the edges of the shaded windows.

"I'm going over to the Hollenden," Ness said, rising, yawning, tightening his tie just a bit. "I'm going to catch a couple of hours' sleep before the Grand Jury session convenes."

The men trudged out, tired to the bone, uncertain to a man about just what, if anything, had been accomplished on this long night.

16

The next night, crowding ten, the same four men—Eliot Ness, Robert Chamberlin, Will Garner, and Albert Curry—sat at a booth in the lounge of the Hollenden Hotel. It was the same booth in which, months before, Ness had held court with various members of the Cleveland press, announcing his intentions to launch a numbers-racket inquiry. The walnut-appointed lounge had a low-key atmosphere, with subdued lighting to match. The mood of these men, however, was neither low-key nor subdued.

The nation's most famous former Prohibition agent was pouring to overflowing the other three detectives' upraised champagne glasses with the appropriate bubbly beverage. The men were all smiles—even Garner, who prided himself on his stoic Indian countenance, was grinning like a C student who just got straight As.

Ness, grinning at least as wide as any other man at the table, poured himself some champagne and they clinked glasses.

"To Salvatore Lombardi," Ness said. "Wherever he is."

Everyone laughed. This was a good sign, considering the escape of Lombardi was easily the biggest stain on their victory. Word on the street was that Lombardi had skipped town; that he had headed south, figuratively and literally. Mexico, it was said.

Even without Lombardi's presence at the Grand Jury today, there was much to celebrate. Indictments had indeed come down on all twenty-three numbers racketeers; only five were still at large. Even without Lombardi and Scalise in custody, the Mayfield Road mob's hold on the numbers racket was broken. The boys couldn't run the racket from jail or from Mexico or whatever rathole the likes of Scalise had dug himself.

And one key figure—slot-machine king Albert "Chuck" Polizzi, peer of Lombardi and Scalise—had sauntered into the Hollenden lounge earlier this afternoon, when Ness was at lunch.

"Sit down, Chuck," Ness had said. "I'll buy you a drink."

Nattily dressed in a cream-color summer suit, darkly tanned, the forty-five-year-old gangster had grinned smugly and slid into the booth next to the safety director.

"I been in Florida," Chuck Polizzi said cockily. "Fishin'. Spending' time with the wife and kids. Flew back when I heard you guys was interested in talkin' to me."

"You were indicted this morning," Ness said.

Dark-haired, bright-eyed Polizzi shrugged, smirked, and had a bourbon and Coke, on Ness. Chuck Polizzi had done time for armed robbery, once, long ago; but more recently had beaten rap after rap. He obviously thought he had no reason to worry. But Ness, knowing the witnesses and the evidence, knew better. Polizzi would finally do his second stretch.

Ness had spent the morning with the Grand Jury, of course, and the afternoon on the phone to friends at the FBI, who had promised to arrest any of the five who fled, under the new federal fugitive law that made it a crime to cross a state line to avoid felony charges.

He'd also had a visit from Reverend Hollis of the Future Outlook League. Again, Hollis did not have an appointment, but Ness didn't care: He was eager to see the race leader. The victories of the day faded, momentarily, and the anger of the early-morning hours had returned like a chronic injury that flared up in bad weather.

But Hollis was angry, too.

"You're to be congratulated, obviously," Hollis said tightly, "on your success with the Grand Jury this morning."

"Thank you. Will you have a seat?"

"Thank you, no. I won't be here that long, Mr. Ness."

That may have been a tactic, Ness realized; the preacher, imposing in clerical black, was taller than the safety director and was looking down at him with condescension masquerading as righteousness.

"You did much damage last night," Hollis said, in a clipped, clearly angry fashion. "That raid at the Democratic League was the poorest possible public-relations move you could have made."

Ness was astounded. "What?"

"You've made yourself look extremely bad in the Negro community—white cops harassing some of the east side's finer citizens. The white press has given you a free ride, but the *Call and Post* will crucify you. I only hope it won't damage your ability to hang on to your witnesses in the coming trial."

Ness resisted the urge to remind the good Reverend that the "finer citizens" of the east side who were arrested last night included a man who engaged in a sex act on stage, as well as many of the enthusiastic audience members who had cheered him on.

Instead, Ness said, "Good God, man—the tip came from you, didn't it?"

Now it was Hollis's turn to look startled.

"Hell, no!" the clergyman said.

"Hell no?" Ness asked.

Hollis looked at Ness warily. "Frankly, that might have been a tactic my friend Councilman Raney would approve of—in a weak moment—but I have enough common sense to assess the ramifications of such a foolhardy enterprise."

Hollis always sounded like he was giving a sermon, Ness noted; and it was getting goddamn irritating.

Ness pointed a lecturing finger at the preacher—he didn't poke him with it, or shake it in his face; but he did point.

He said, "We had a call from one of your Future Outlook League members. Look in your own backyard, Reverend, if you want somebody to blame."

Hollis thought about that for a moment, then his eyes squinted behind his wire-frame glasses as he said, "Which member called? Did he give a name?"

"Well, no."

"Then how do you know it really was one of my members? Perhaps you should look in your *own* backyard, Mr. Ness."

There was an awkward moment then, as both men realized the anger they had brought into this impromptu meeting was ill-placed. Hollis nodded and twitched a smile of farewell; they did not shake hands before the preacher left.

That one, odd encounter had been the only inglorious moment in a great day for Eliot Ness and his staff.

"Cullitan's going to ask that bail be set at fifty grand per defendant," Ness said, between sips of champagne. "Except for Willie the Emperor—he's worth one hundred and fifty."

Curry smiled and shook his head. "Think the prosecutor can pull that off? That'd be an all-time record for a criminal case in this county."

"I think so," Ness said. "Judge Walther is one of the honest ones."

"Here's to Judge Walther," Chamberlin said, raising his glass, and the rest of the men followed suit, clinked, drank.

Ness glanced up and saw a big black man in a baggy brown suit moving quickly through the lounge, carrying a battered black fedora in one hand like a dead rat to be dumped in a garbage can. Most of the all-white patrons of the Hollenden lounge looked at Toussaint Johnson as if a rat were exactly what he was carrying.

"Detective Johnson," Ness said pleasantly. "Sit down and join us—have some champagne."

Toussaint Johnson shook his head, no. His harshly handsome face looked like a carved African mask; his eyes were intense and troubled.

"Bad shit happening in Central-Scovill," he said.

"Sit," Ness said. This time it wasn't a request.

Johnson squeezed in next to Curry; the men were watching the Negro cop with rapt attention: None of them had ever seen him this close to upset before.

"There's a flyin' squad of dago hoodlums racing around the east side," Johnson said. "Offering cash money."

"Huh?" Ness said.

Johnson breathed out heavily and started over. "Four hoods nobody ever seen before is driving all over the east side in a black Buick, offering five hundred bucks cold cash to anybody who'll cough up the name of any one of our seventy secret witnesses."

"Damn," Ness said.

"That's a lot of money," Curry said breathlessly.

"You think that's a lot of money in the Hollenden Hotel," Johnson said, " 'magine what it is on the east side."

"I wonder if they're getting any takers," Chamberlin said.

"I don't know," Johnson said. "But it gets worse 'fore it gets better, and it don't get better." He paused for effect. "They're offering a *thousand* clams for the *whereabouts* of any witness."

All of the men looked at Ness.

Minor witnesses were holed up in the YMCA, with considerable police protection. But key witnesses were hidden away in a safe house whose location was known only to Ness and his closest safety department associates—Chamberlin, Curry, and Garner—and the handful of crack rookie uniform cops that Ness had hand-picked to stand guard there.

"*Ten* thousand bucks wouldn't spring that information loose," Ness said confidently. "Nobody on the east side even knows the 'whereabouts.' "

Since that was supposed to include Johnson himself, the big Negro cop said, in a barely audible tone, "The projects."

The Outhwaite public housing project was a relatively new

addition to the east side and one partially completed building, into which tenants weren't due to move for several months, was indeed where Ness was sequestering his key witnesses.

Ness flinched, as if a punch had been thrown. "How in hell . . . ?"

"Ain't much on the east side that I don't know," Johnson said flatly. "And what I don't know, I can figure out."

"And if you know . . ."

"I ain't the only smart colored man in Cleveland, Mr. Ness."

"What do you suggest, Detective Johnson?"

"I suggest we put together a couple of flyin' squads of our own, and go prowlin' the Roarin' Third looking for a black sedan that don't have cops in it."

Ness was already getting up. "That, Detective Johnson, is a fine idea."

Curry, Johnson, and Chamberlin piled into the Negro detective's second-hand Chevy, while Ness and Garner took the EN-1 sedan. Garner, who had lived undercover on the east side for nearly a month in the earliest stages of the investigation, was familiar enough with the territory to guide the way; he in fact drove, while Ness kept an eye out.

It was a Wednesday night, colder than the night before, but the way the streets of the Roaring Third were hopping, it might've been Saturday. Jukeboxes exploded with uptempo music inside saloons burning with neon; colored men in every range of apparel from rags to zoot suits milled up and down the sidewalks, their boisterous voices spanning every human emotion, laughing, shouting, raging; whores decorated street corners and in the recessions of doorways junkies sat on cement steps like potted plants, only babbling. Ness noted with clinical interest the businesses that were undoubtedly numbers drops: tobacco stands, barber shops, newsstands—these wouldn't likely be open at eleven-something at night, otherwise. While he rode, studying this street of barbecue stands, bars, and bedbug-haven hotels, Ness flashed an order over the police radio to pick up the four hoods in the black sedan. Garner kept prowling. They were on Central, now, in the east fifties.

"Something," Garner said, taking one hand off the wheel to point up ahead.

It was a black sedan, its tail sticking out of an alley, revealing a mud-spattered license plate. The doors were open.

"Pull over," Ness said, needlessly, because Garner already was.

Ness jumped out of the car, just as it was stopping, and reached absent-mindedly for his gun. All he touched was the empty shoulder holster: He hadn't taken time to fill it.

No matter. The car, a new Buick parked in the middle of an alley next to a dignified two-story brick undertaking parlor, was empty.

Garner had a look inside the car. "Registered to Roland Rushing."

"That's the Emperor's brother. Go call it in, Will—have him picked up."

Ness walked down the alley a ways, not looking for anything in particular. A cat scurried across his path and made him jump, a little. As the darkness of the alley gathered in on him, he suddenly became aware that he was walking unarmed down a ghetto alley, next to a funeral home. He felt a hand on his shoulder, and turned quickly, ready to swing.

"Easy, boss," Garner said.

Ness sighed heavily. "Gave me a start."

"Carry a gun. You'll live longer. We got trouble—come on."

Ness followed his old comrade out of the alley, as Garner's words flew out in an uncharacteristic rush: "I was getting ready to put that APB out on Roland Rushing when I heard the call."

They were to their sedan, now.

"What call?"

Garner, on the driver's side, looked gravely across the top of the car at Ness, standing on the rider's side. "The dispatcher said Mrs. John C. Washington called for help—four men broke into her home looking for her husband."

"Damn! Was she hurt?"

"Don't know."

"Get the hell over there right now."

The Hawthorne Avenue area felt even more like a trap tonight, as they turned back east past the fortress-like wall of factories, into the quiet neighborhood where the John C. Washington home had once again been invaded.

Two uniformed patrolmen were inside with the former policy king's queen; one of them stood near Mrs. Washington, who wore a pink satin robe, as she sat on the couch, crying into a handkerchief. The other cop was in the kitchen, applying a damp cloth to the head of a burly fiftyish Negro in sportcoat and no tie, the Washingtons' live-in bodyguard.

The living room had been turned upside-down; not as thorough a job as when the cops had played wrecking crew here a few months before. But thorough enough.

Ness sat next to Mrs. Washington. The slightly plump, very pretty woman looked up with a tear-streaked face, her mouth quivering, her eyes red and frightened and angry.

"We just got this place put back the way it should be," she said, as hurt as a disappointed child, as bitter as a spurned lover.

"Yes, I know," Ness said. "I'm sorry. I wish you would've let us post men here, like I asked."

"Johnny didn't want that. He said that'd tip everybody off that he was talking. We have bodyguards anyway. That oughta been enough."

"Yes, it should. But we'll protect you from here on out."

She was shaking her head emphatically. "I'm tired of this, I'm so tired of this . . . first you damn white police ruin my beautiful house, then more white men, *criminals* this time, come do the same blessed thing. You're all the damn same. Ain't no difference between you. White crooks, white cops, what's the difference?"

"I know it must seem that way to you, Mrs. Washington."

Sometimes it seemed that way to Ness. He'd put as many cops in jail as gangsters, in this town.

He squeezed her shoulder gently. "But it wasn't anybody white who sold you out, tonight."

She blinked, cocked her head. "What do you mean?"

"Those same four men who worked you over were riding around the east side earlier this evening, offering money for the names of witnesses."

Her features tightened. "You're saying, someone of my race took money to give up Johnny C.?"

"Most likely."

She sat and blankly stared.

"What exactly happened here, Mrs. Washington?"

She didn't say anything for a while, but Ness didn't repeat his question. He waited patiently for her to respond. Finally, she did.

"Four men—white men, dago men. Big awful men. One of them must have knocked out Milton."

She meant the bodyguard.

"They come in demanding to talk to Johnny C.," she continued. "I told them Johnny was out of town on business, like we been saying. They looked all over the house, busting stuff up." She began to cry again. He patted her shoulder. "They said . . . they said . . . 'we'll be back.' "

Ness looked up at Garner. Garner lifted his eyebrows.

"They probably will," Ness said. "I'm going to move you in with your husband."

"Oh, I'd like that. I'd like that very much."

"We're going to put an end to this," he said.

She was shaking her head again. "I don't know what Johnny C. is going to do when he hears about this."

"I hope," Ness said, "that he says he'll go along with what I have in mind. . . ."

17

Little Angelo Scalise, not a perfect specimen of mental health even under the best of conditions, was about to go fucking nuts.

He had been living in the small cement hide-out room behind the lanes at Pla-Mor bowling alley for more than two days now. When Black Sal got tipped that indictments were about to hit the fan, Scalise had holed up in the cement-block room that Lombardi and his associates had used since Prohibition days as a cool-off flat. The room was tiny—a cubicle really—with only one window, and that consisted of glass bricks you couldn't see out of, and a cot and a small dresser and a tiny ice-box and a hot plate and a little Bakelite radio. It wasn't a hell of a lot better than a prison cell.

And in a prison cell, you wouldn't have to listen to the constant racket of clattering bowling pins.

The noise was muffled, but not *that* muffled, and Ange flinched involuntarily with every strike. For a guy who loved to bowl, it was a strange sort of hell. On the few times when he stuck his head out, just to fight the fucking closed-in feeling, he'd see those goddamn pin boys in the narrow walk-way area behind the lanes. They'd be laughing and talking, and he couldn't make out what they were saying because of the sound of pins getting knocked over. But he knew those little fuckers were laughing at him. He'd clipped 'em with pins often enough. He would go back in and flop on his cot and shut the door and muffle the sound of clattering pins and contemplate how much fun it would be to bash in those little fuckers' brains with a bowling pin.

His cousin Sal had gone south—he'd be in Acapulco by now, spread out on the beach like a big dead fucking fish. They had money in a resort hotel down there, so Sal would be living like a king. But not like a man.

For all Sal's talk of how important respect was, the fat slob was nothing but a coward, turning his back on a fucking five-mil-a-year business, just because Eliot fucking Ness lined up some niggers to squeal. Angelo wasn't about to turn his back on such a business, to walk away from his money and his manhood.

"We're rich men," Lombardi had told him, before catching the chartered plane. "We've worked long and hard. Our fathers worked long and hard. We can afford to take a rest, a vacation for a while. Few years pass, this'll all blow over."

"I ain't gonna waste the best years of my life loafin' on some Mexican beach, with some Mexican bitch sucking my dick! What kind of life is that for a man?"

Sal had contemplated that, and said, "Not a bad one at all," and got on the plane.

Goddamn him!

Well, fine. Who the fuck needed him. Angelo would have the whole goddamn business to himself. Sal and Polizzi and the others were acting like this was the end of the damn world, or at least the damn numbers racket. Hell, as long as there were niggers, there'd be numbers! And as long as there was numbers, there'd be big bucks to be made, and as long as there was big bucks to be made, the Mayfield Road gang— with Little Angelo Scalise as top man, from now on—would own the east side.

All it would take, he knew, was bumping off one of the big witnesses. Bump 'em off big and bloody. It couldn't just be anybody: It had to be somebody with a name in Central-

Scovill. Then those niggers would turn their black tails and run.

Scalise's laughter echoed in the little cement room. Pins clattered out on the lanes. He flinched.

Before he'd gone into hiding, he called on some freelance torpedoes from Detroit, who were part of the old Purple Gang. Two brothers, Harry and Sam Keenan, who it was said worked look-out in the St. Valentine's Day massacre back in Chicago in '29, and a fellow named Greene and another named Berns. They were all Jews, but Scalise didn't give a fuck. He wasn't prejudiced.

The Keenan brothers had done jobs for Scalise before— including an important early hit in the Mayfield Road numbers takeover. It was the Keenans who blew Rufus Murphy all to shit in his driveway back in '33. They did good work. Not cheap—they were Jews after all—but value for the dollar. And tough bastards—they wouldn't talk if you fed their nuts to 'em one at a time.

Angelo had turned the Keenans and Greene and Berns loose on the east side last night. Waving fat wads of cash under nigger noses, looking for Ness witnesses. But they hadn't got anywhere, and—at Angelo's suggestion—went on to the home of Johnny C., a policy king who "retired" when Ange turned up the heat a few years back. Ange figured Johnny C.—who word on the street said was "out of town, on business"—was a sure bet to be one of Ness's sequestered witnesses.

So the Keenans and company shook the house down and Mrs. Washington up. Then—also at Angelo's suggestion— one of them, Greene, hung around the neighborhood, staking out the house. Sure enough, first the cops showed, then Ness himself, and pretty soon Johnny C. shows, too, chauffeured by that hard-ass coon cop Toussaint Johnson. The place was crawling with uniformed cops and plainclothes dicks, so there was no way Greene could make a play for Washington.

But when Washington came out of the house—looking like nigger royalty in his fancy English suit with black-and-white shoes and homburg hat—with a white uniformed cop as his driver, Greene tailed them and saw the cop escort Johnny C. to the Outhwaite public housing project, barely two blocks away.

Imagine that fucking Ness, hiding his witnesses out right there on the east side, close to home but out of sight, minutes from downtown and the courthouse. Scalise had to give the guy his balls, and his brains. Outhwaite was perfect, in a crazy way. The housing project was finished but for a central, X-shaped building that was supposed to be ready for residents in a couple months. Chances were Ness had all his key witnesses in that one, new, nearly finished building.

But all Scalise needed was Washington. Johnny C. was a *name* on the east side; he was still a powerful businessman, respected and even feared. If Johnny C. couldn't make it to the witness stand without dying, nobody else would risk it either; all that Ness talk in the papers about "safety in numbers" and "protection from reprisals" would look like the bullshit it was.

And the numbers racket would be up and running again, in the hands of the Mayfield Road gang, under the leadership of one Little Angelo Scalise. Only maybe from now on it would be "Big" Angelo.

Today Scalise had sent the Purple Gang boys to hole up in a hotel in Warrensville Heights, while he sent for Freddy Douglass, the Frank Hogey policy controller into whom Ange had put a scare some months ago in the alley by the Elite Cabaret.

Freddy, who liked his fancy clothes and fancy women, was hurting, thanks to Ness and his policy-racket squeeze. Scalise gave him a grand in twenties to play with at the Outhwaite housing project.

"Find out which building Washington's in," Ange told him, "and you earn a C-note. Find out the apartment number, and you earn a grand. And either way, you can keep the change."

"You got it, Mr. Scalise," Freddy said, putting the money

in the jacket of his snappy gray suit. The small cement cubicle in the back of the bowling alley seemed like a closet with two men in it, and the smell of Freddy's heavy cologne made Scalise a little sick.

But Scalise knew Freddy was a good boy, one of the best of the colored crew, maybe *the* best of those who didn't get caught up in Ness's numbers net.

"Careful, now, Fred," Scalise said, ushering him out. "There's gonna be plenty of cops around. Could be plainclothes. Dress down . . . look like somebody who might live in the projects."

"They dress good over there, Mr. Scalise. You got to pass certain requirements to get in there."

Scalise snorted a laugh. "I thought 'poor' and 'colored' was all it took."

"No. You can't get in if you got a record. I oughta know: I tried. Those are nice flats."

"Better than this shithole I'm stuck in," Scalise said, with a smirk, and patted the Negro on the back, sending him on his way.

That had been this morning. At two in the afternoon he got a call from Freddy, who had the info.

"He's in the center building," Freddy said quickly. "That X-shaped building."

Just as Scalise had figured.

"That part was easy," Freddy went on. "I just asked around—cost me a double-sawbuck, is all. But I also finagled you the apartment number."

"Beautiful, kid! Give."

"Johnny's on the top floor. It's five stories, and he's in 514. Nobody up on top but witnesses and probably some cops standing guard. There's no cops on the grounds, that I could see, anyway."

"Makes sense," Ange said. "They don't wanna advertise—but there's cops there, all right."

"Up on the fifth floor there's got to be. I had a hell of a time gettin' this. I don't think nobody livin' at Outhwaite has got this info.''

"How the hell did you manage it, boy?"

"There's some white workmen, finishin' up that building. Painters and carpenters. Good union guys who don't like cops.''

"That's nice work, Freddy. You didn't leave a trail, did you?''

"Naw. I said I had a hundred bucks from a reporter to find out where Johnny C. was being kept. Said I'd split it with anybody interested.''

"You did good, boy. Made out like a bandit, on that grand I gave you. I'm gonna leave your fifteen hundred in a paper bag at the bar with Louie. Pick up it after closing—they don't serve coloreds here.''

There was a slight pause, then: "Fine, boss.''

Ange had next phoned Harry Keenan at the hotel in Warrensville Heights.

"Go buy an old used delivery truck,'' he told Keenan. "Pay cash and use a phony name. Make sure it runs good, though. Then get a couple of them tin tool kits—big enough to stuff our heaters in. And find some second-hand shop where you can buy coveralls and work clothes, loose-fitting so we can wear regular street clothes under.''

"We?''

"Yeah. I'm coming along. I wouldn't miss this for the fuckin' world.''

Ange had been cooped up in his cement cell too long—just two days, really, but it seemed forever—and besides, he wanted the word to go out that he did this deed himself. Angelo Scalise himself put the bullets in that squealing nigger Washington.

That would earn him respect. Like his cousin Sal professed, but didn't live up to, respect was all-important in a business like this. The whole east side—the whole damn town—would know you don't fuck with Angelo Scalise, the big boss of the Mayfield Road gang.

He let the Keenans and Greene and Berns in the back, up the fire escape, and they all changed clothes in his little closet of a room. Harry Keenan, a big guy who looked like a melancholy bear, said he had silencers for the guns.

"No silencers," Ange said, placing a .45 automatic and a .38 revolver, both Colts, in a steel-gray tool kit that contained nothing else except two boxes of ammunition and some towels stuffed in to keep the guns from rattling around. "I want the world to hear this."

"This place could be crawling with cops," Greene said. Both he and his partner Berns were burly, with lumpy anonymous faces. Sam Keenan rarely said a word; he was a skinny pale killer with a pointy chin and nose, and seemed always to follow his brother's lead.

"There's gonna be cops," Ange admitted, "but it won't be crawlin' with 'em. They can't afford to, it'd give 'em away."

"Killing cops ain't a brilliant idea," Berns said. "Remember the shit storm after the Kansas City massacre?"

Ange waved that off. "That was feds, and besides, we're just gonna kill a nigger. We won't kill any cops unless they get in the way. Shoot 'em in the kneecaps, why don't you? If you're squeamish."

Harry Keenan planted himself in the middle of the small cement room and spread his hands like an umpire. With five men in there, it was as crowded as the stateroom scene in that Marx Brothers movie. And Ange didn't like being crowded.

"We need big dough for this," Keenan said. "We never bargained for going head-on with cops. You want us to risk puttin' our faces in every post office in the country with state, feds, and locals aiming to put our asses in the hot squat, you'd better up the fuckin' ante, Ange."

"You want me to up the fuckin' ante? I'll up your fuckin' ante." Angelo felt the red rising into his face. "You can fucking *retire* when this is over. A hundred grand apiece. Is that the fuck enough for you bozos?"

The men glanced at each other with eyes wide with dollar signs and, slowly, began to nod. One hundred thousand depression dollars would buy these men a new life. And these aging remnants of the once-proud Purple Gang could use an opportunity like that, to hell with the risks.

"Agreed," Harry said, for all of them.

The Outhwaite housing project was bordered on the north by Quincy and the south by Woodland. The five men were in a battered brown '34 Reo panel truck, Harry and Angelo in the front, the rest riding in back. All wore work clothes— coveralls and caps.

"Anybody asks," Ange had told them all, "we're plumbers. But let me do the talkin'."

A second car, a four-door Plymouth, was parked on a side street off Quincy, a few blocks away, so on the getaway they could dump the panel truck with the work clothes inside. Right now, just after four o'clock, they pulled into the access road that took them between two large red-and-orange brick buildings and into the large grassy courtyard of the projects. Outhwaite was like a fortress, a rectangle of land between 40th and 55th with rows of modern brick apartment buildings on each side; in the center was the nearly finished X-shaped building where Washington was sequestered.

The afternoon was cool and overcast, but not cold; colored kids of grade-school age with light jackets or no jackets were running around the big grassy area, playing kick the can, screaming gleefully. Several trucks of various sizes, apparently belonging to the handful of white workmen who were milling about, were parked on the grass near the X-shaped building. Up on the roof were more white laborers, working with tar; the smell of it was in the air.

Angelo and his four cohorts got out of the panel truck slowly, casually, talking amongst themselves—the topic of conversation being whether that Iowa kid Bob Feller could pitch the Indians into the next World Series.

A young-looking fair-haired workman loading a ladder into the back of a truck said, "Hiya," and then, "Little late in the day to be comin' to work, ain't it, fellas?"

"You know how it is in the plumbing business," Ange

said, shrugging, fist tightening around the handle of the tin tool box he was lugging. "Trouble with those new fixtures already."

"No rest for the wicked," the workman said with a grin, and went back about his own business.

The double doors to the main lobby were in the middle of the X on the Woodland Avenue side. The lobby was unfinished cement, ceiling and floor, and empty. Angelo tried the elevator, but it wasn't working yet. They found a stairwell and walked up, flight after flight, without a word.

At the landing of the fifth floor, Angelo paused and peeked out the hallway door.

Not a soul in sight.

Like the lobby, the walls were concrete and so was the floor, no carpet or tile laid yet. The light fixtures had not been put in, though bulbs and wiring were in place. The place smelled new: The scents of fresh cement, of glue, of metal, mingled. There were, however, numbers on the varnished wood doors.

Angelo posted Greene on the stairwell door. He sent Berns to the other end of the hall, cautioning both men not to create a crossfire if any gunplay broke out. Then Ange led the Keenans down the hallway to room 514. Harry, like Ange, was hauling a tin tool kit. Carefully, quietly, both men set their tool kits on the floor, snapped them open, and withdrew guns. Harry took out two nine-millimeter Brownings, kept one, and gave one to his skeletal brother Sam; Ange held his Colts, the .45 and the .38, in either hand, a regular two-gun plumber. With nods, he positioned Harry and Sam on either side of the door, their backs to the cement wall.

Whispering, just mouthing the words really, he told them, "Follow me."

Then Ange raised his foot and kicked the door in with one try, knocking the fucker off its hinges.

He bulled through, into a barely furnished living room, and, seeing a figure in a chair by a window with its back turned, he began shooting with both hands. Harry and Sam

Keenan burst into the room and followed Ange's lead, bullets chewing up the sparse second-hand furnishings and punching holes in newly plastered walls and shattering the glass of windows that overlooked the grassy courtyard. The sound bounced off the hard plastered walls, flattening but not muting it; the din was deafening. The air filled with cordite and smoke and powdered plaster from the walls.

It was all over in a matter of seconds.

The three men stood flat-footed for a moment, watching the store-window dummy in the English suit tumble out of the chair, shot to shit.

From an adjoining room at left, possibly the kitchen, Eliot Ness emerged, with his own .38 in hand; from a room at the right, possibly a bedroom, Toussaint Johnson came out with a shiny silver revolver in either hand. Angelo was not the only two-gun cowboy in this corral.

"Just drop them," Ness said.

"*I* know *you*," Johnson said, his eyes narrowing, his nostrils flaring, pointing accusingly first at Sam and then at Harry Keenan with each of the silver weapons.

At once Angelo and the two Keenans knew exactly who Johnson was and what he meant: That this was the Negro detective who had been at the scene of the murder of Rufus Murphy; the man who had in fact pursued Sam Keenan through Murphy's backyard on that violent night in 1933. In a flash all three men knew that they were facing the black cop whose friend they had killed.

So nobody dropped their gun.

Instead the Keenans stepped forward to fire at Johnson, faces taut with desperation, but Johnson beat them to it; he was screaming with rage as he fired both those silver revolvers simultaneously, aiming one at Harry and one at Sam, who were on either side of the stunned Angelo, punching a hole through the chest of Sam and another through the forehead of Harry, whose head came apart like a melon. Out of the corner of Ange's left eye he saw most of the inside of Harry's head go *splat* against the wall, like a mudball flung by a kid, a bloody gray mess sliding down the plaster wall.

Ange turned tail and ran.

But in the hall, down at their respective ends, both Greene and Berns were in the custody of workmen—or cops dressed as workmen, anyway.

There was nothing else Ange could do: He shot Greene in the head and the cop had a dead guy in his arms and brains in his face when Ange rushed past, rocketing down the stairs.

"Scalise!"

The voice echoing down the stairwell was one he recognized: that fucker Ness. Ange kept running; three steps at a time. Behind him he could hear the sound of somebody hurtling down the stairs, the footsteps on top of each other, applause-like.

That fucker Ness.

He could stop and shoot it out, but better to get outside, where there were nigger babies playing and the cops wouldn't dare shoot. His heart was pounding against his chest when he reached the doorway at the bottom of the stairs. Ness was right behind him, a flight behind him—but if he could get through the lobby, shoot his way through if there were cops there, to the outside, to the truck or even to where he could run between buildings and out to the street, take a hostage if he had to, some little darkie he could haul around like a rag doll, then he was home free. . . .

The lobby was still empty and he ran out into the cool afternoon, a gun in either hand, and something hit him in the chest. He stopped dead in his tracks.

Literally.

Will Garner, dressed like a carpenter, stood over Angelo's corpse, smoke curling out his revolver's barrel.

Ness was out the door a moment later, and knelt over the body, felt for a pulse in the neck. Sighed and stood.

"Right through the pump," Ness said.

"I know," Garner said blandly.

Toussaint Johnson bolted out the door, stopped dead in his tracks—figuratively—and looked down at Angelo's body.

"Who nailed him?" Johnson said, emotionlessly.

Ness nodded toward Garner.

"Nice goin'," Johnson said. To Ness he said, "Sorry it got out of hand up there."

"Not your fault," Ness said, putting his own gun back in its shoulder holster. "They called it, not us."

Johnson gestured upward with a thumb. "Those boys I drilled upstairs—they're the triggers who hit Rufus Murphy, years ago. I recognized the skinny one."

"The Keenan brothers," Ness said, nodding. "Purple Gang. Done a lot of freelance work over the years, including a hand in the St. Valentine's Day job, if rumor's right."

"No shit," Johnson said. He put his silver guns away and yawned. "I could use a meal 'bout now."

Ness just looked at him. Albert Curry, dressed in work clothes, came walking up, had a look at the corpse and smiled tightly.

"Rest for the wicked after all," Curry said, quietly.

"Come on, fellas," Johnson said. He grinned at Ness. "I'm buyin'. Who's for gumbo?"

18

Eliot Ness spent the morning of the first of May—a beautiful, sunny Monday—cooped up in court. And he didn't mind one bit.

Judge Hurd, presiding in the criminal branch of Common Pleas Court, refused to lower the $50,000-per-man bond under which the policy racketeers were being held at County Jail—except for Willie "the Emperor" Rushing, of course, who rated $150,000. The various attorneys for the various defendants reiterated their mutual contention that the size of the bail was unconstitutional. But Judge Hurd completely backed up Judge Walther, who on Saturday had set the bail when the suspects to a man pleaded not guilty to extorting money by force from numbers-game operators.

All of that was first thing Monday morning; by mid-morning Ness was in another courtroom, watching the arraignment of Frank Hogey, the white policy king whose sleazy smugness had finally evaporated. Hogey, dressed in an expensively tailored suit but nervous, his hands twitching, lips trembling, listened glumly as his lawyer spoke on his behalf.

A less reliable judge than Hurd or Walther had slapped Hogey on the wrist with a fine, when Ness had made that big numbers haul the previous year. Today would be different.

Hogey, who'd been vacationing at Hot Springs, Arkansas, had surrendered himself over the weekend, at Central Jail, where he demanded to see Ness. The safety director, relaxing at his boathouse with Ev MacMillan, declined to drive into the city, but agreed to speak to Hogey on the phone.

"Mr. Ness," Hogey said, his desperation unhidden. "Couldn't we work something out? You said something about immunity, if I testified . . ."

"I don't need your testimony anymore, Frank. Scalise is dead, and Lombardi went south. And we got testimony and evidence enough on the rest of you to last till Christ comes back."

Hogey's voice exploded with frustration. "Jesus, how the hell was I supposed to know you'd pull off this goddamn harebrained investigation?"

"You gambled, Frank. You lost."

And Ness, with a great deal of satisfaction, had hung up.

This morning, in court, Hogey's attorney had described his client as a large property holder, the proprietor of meat markets, cafés, restaurants, and a former bail bondsman himself. "We don't deny Mr. Hogey has operated gambling games to some extent, but we do deny he ever extorted money from anybody. A bond of $10,000 would be more than adequate."

But the judge hit Hogey with the by-now standard $50,000, anyway.

And Ness had sat in court, arms folded, smiling to himself, feeling like the cat that ate every goddamn canary in town.

Despite his canary feast, he'd taken his inner circle— Chamberlin, Garner, and Curry—out to lunch. No champagne, but he did pick up the tab. After they'd eaten, the ebullient men had a couple of drinks.

"I've asked the U.S. Immigration Bureau to help us hunt for the missing fugitives," Ness said.

"You still hold out hope to bag Lombardi?" Chamberlin asked.

"As long as I'm safety director, he'll stay a prime target. We're already talking to the Mexican authorities."

"Good," Garner said.

"And we're going to keep the heat turned up on the east

side. Various Mayfield Road lieutenants are scurrying around the Roaring Third, trying to carry on for their departed bosses. We have to make sure they don't get a foothold."

"Then what?" Curry said.

"Then," Ness said, sipping his Scotch, "we get on about our business. We have bigger and better crimes to tend to than persecuting small-fry Negro policy operators."

"Do I smell the subtle perfume of politics?" Chamberlin said, a wry little smile curving under the military mustache, as he lit up his ever-present pipe.

"You smell your own damn fumes," Ness said cheerfully. "And you smell reality." Ness sipped his drink, raised an eyebrow. "With the Mayfield Road mob out of business, the numbers racket just isn't a major concern of the department of public safety anymore."

Curry was swirling his drink, a bourbon and water. "Maybe that's not such a bad thing."

"What?" Chamberlin asked.

"You know what I mean," Curry said, shrugging. "Leaving the east side Negro community alone, where that's concerned. For a lot of 'em, the numbers is the only hope they got in a hopeless life."

No one said anything.

Ness smiled one-sidedly and said, "Albert, that doesn't sound like you. You usually see problems in terms of black and white."

"No," Curry said, shaking his head. "I've always seen problems in terms of *white*. We all have."

That sobered everyone, but not in a bad way; everyone was smiling, albeit faintly.

Then Garner said, "What you mean 'we,' paleface?" and the table broke up into laughter.

"Albert," Ness said, "you seem older, all of a sudden— maybe it's being a sergeant that's done it."

Curry looked at Ness curiously. "A what?"

"A sergeant," he said. "If you pass the exam, that is.

Here's to Sergeant Albert Curry, Department of Public Safety.''

Ness raised his glass to the suddenly grinning Curry and the other men raised their glasses and smiled and general congratulations were passed around.

Now Ness was back at his office, and he had one other member of his team to deal with. At two-thirty, right on time, Detective Toussaint Johnson was shown into the safety director's office. Johnson held his misshapen charcoal fedora in one hand; his angularly handsome face was a blank slate. He looked considerably different than he had when, dressed in John C. Washington's finery, he led the bad guys from Washington's house to Outhwaite, where a trap was being laid.

"Sit down, Detective," Ness said, pleasant but business-like. Ness was standing, gesturing to the nearby conference table.

Johnson nodded, and sat. Ness stood nearby. Even standing over him, Ness felt the massive presence of the big colored cop. This was not a man who could be easily intimidated.

"I've been searching my soul," Ness admitted, "about what to do with you."

Johnson thought for a moment, before calmly saying, "What you mean, Mr. Ness?"

"I mean you're a good cop. One of the best I've worked with in Cleveland."

Johnson grinned easily. "Is that what white folks call damnin' with faint praise, Mr. Ness?"

Ness didn't grin back. "Not really. There are quite a few good cops in this town. But, I'll admit, not many in your class."

"You mean, colored?"

"No. I mean, good. Dedicated. Hard. I want to promote you, Toussaint."

Johnson sat up; the surprise registered only in his eyes, but it registered.

Ness sat on the edge of the conference table. "Only I have

a problem. You did a fine job on this numbers racketeering case. We couldn't have done it without you. No question of that.''

"Thanks.''

"I've already put you in for a certificate of commendation, and a medal of valor.''

"Well. Thanks, again.''

"No thanks necessary. You earned both, in spades.''

Johnson's lips quivered with amusement.

Then Ness realized what he'd said, and, embarrassed, added, "You know what I mean.''

"Yes, sir.''

"And a promotion would certainly be appropriate. I've put Albert Curry in for promotion, to sergeant, for his work on this case.''

"He got it coming.''

"No more than you. Not as much as you, frankly.''

"Well . . .''

"He's white? Sure he is. But that's not why I promoted him, without having to dedicate one moment to soul-searching. You see, Albert's loyalty is unquestioned. His integrity you could bounce rocks off.''

Johnson shifted in his chair; he swallowed thickly. Something approaching anger was building behind his eyes. "What are you sayin', Mr. Ness?''

"I'm saying you held out on me, Toussaint. You knew Clifford Willis was a dirty cop. You knew that was why he got bumped off by the Mayfield bunch. You knew that he used to be Johnny C.'s bagman. You knew that was why his brother officers rushed to his presumed defense, smashing up Johnny C.'s castle. And you didn't tell me. I had to find out elsewhere. I had to find out from a goddamn snitch.''

Johnson's anger never got off the ground; his eyes went hooded, as if he were sleepy. He seemed more weary than ashamed. If he felt any shame. Ness couldn't tell.

He tried to find out. "What do you say to that, Toussaint?''

Johnson sighed; he moved his head on his neck like it

weighed more than the rest of him put together. "Mr. Ness—I told you when we first talked, I used to work for Rufus Murphy. You knew I wasn't no angel. But you didn't ask me no questions about whether I was ever on the pad or not. You know why you didn't ask?"

Ness paused. Then he said, "Why?"

" 'Cause you didn't want to know."

Ness said nothing.

Toussaint went on: "I wasn't hiding anything from you. I just didn't want either one of us to have to come to terms with why I knew what I knew. That's all."

Ness got up. He sighed heavily. Then he took the hardwood chair next to Johnson and said, "I've already put you in for that promotion."

"What?"

"You're going to be a sergeant, Toussaint, if you can pass the test."

"Hell, I'll pass the damn thing."

"But I'm pulling you out of the Roaring Third."

Johnson backed off, his eyes open very wide. "Well, that's my turf. Shouldn't I oughta be workin' that side of town?"

"From time to time, you will. But if you think I went through these hard months to let a good cop like you give in to temptation, you're crazy."

"Temptation?"

"To go back on the pad. To be the cop who fixes things on the east side for the colored independent policy operators."

Johnson looked like he'd been struck with a plank.

"Toussaint," Ness said, smiling, not hiding the irony in his voice, "you're part of *my* team now. No one can accuse me of race prejudice when I have a Negro detective on my personal staff."

Johnson's eyes were filled with incredulity. "You assigning me permanent to the safety director's office?"

"That's right, Sergeant Johnson."

Ness held out his hand.

"Welcome aboard," Ness said.

Numbly, Johnson shook Ness's hand.

Then Johnson threw back his head and began to laugh, until every pebbled-glass window in the office was rattling.

"And one of these days," Ness said, as he walked the still-chuckling Johnson out, "we're going to nail that bastard Lombardi. He can run . . ."

"But he can't hide," Toussaint Johnson said.

And he wasn't laughing or smiling when he said it.

· EPILOGUE ·

JUNE 2, 1941

19

Black Sal Lombardi sat under the thatched sun shelter on a wooden beach chair, sipping coco-loco from a carved-out coconut. He was watching pretty American girls play soccer with their slightly older American boy friends; they all (Sal, too) wore bathing suits and were soaking up the afternoon sun. He was between Mexican whores right now, having gotten bored with the last girl the hotel man had provided. Sal had been enjoying his privacy these last several days; but watching these golden-tanned American girls bounce and jiggle got him thinking about requesting a new *puta* for this evening.

Playa Caleta was the "morning" beach and most of the tourists headed for Playa Hornos, the "afternoon" beach, after one o'clock. Nobody Sal asked seemed to know why this was—though a few had mentioned tide and shade patterns—but the tradition was long-standing. Sal liked to watch the girls, but he didn't like a crowded beach; so he waited till the afternoon had thinned of tourists before making use of palm-fringed Caleta beach, which his hotel fronted. When he wanted to swim or sun some morning, he used the private pool of his *casita*.

Sal had taken to the sun, though he seldom swam. His olive complexion had gradually baked to a near black, making him truly worthy of the nickname "Black Sal" at last. He had been here, after all, over two years. Two years of vacation or retirement or however you cared to view it.

He knew only that he was happy. His pre-ulcerous condition had gone away; he hadn't had a glass of milk in eighteen months. He weighed ten pounds less and was as physically fit as a teenage boy. At least three times a week, he played the golf course at Playa Encantada—usually with vacationing American businessmen, some of them with ties to his own business—and went fishing several times a month, hiring out a boat and tackle and captain through the hotel. He had sent home several photos of himself with prized catches: sailfish and marlin longer than an elephant's dick. He'd been freshwater fishing in the coastal lagoons, by torch light; he'd gone duck-hunting and once even took a guided expedition into the mountainous interior, where he bagged a mountain lion.

The spectator sports weren't bad, either: Jai alai every night in the *frontón* building near Playa Caleta; bullfights every Sunday afternoon; boxing and wrestling. The nighttime entertainment was wild; from one nightclub you could view a spic kid climb down La Quebrada cliff to a platform and, torch in hand, dive forty feet into a breaker, then climb the opposite cliff to a flat rock one hundred thirty feet up and dive the fuck again, between a narrow sea ravine with jagged rocks on either side. Down below newspapers were set on fire so the kid could see what he was doing. This took balls or no brains or both, but whatever, it was a hell of thing to see.

Sal was glad he had a piece of this action. Acapulco had been just another scenic bay city in the boondocks until the highway was built between here and central Mexico back in '27. Horvitz and some of the other big boys from back home, when Repeal was around the corner, got in on the ground floor when resort hotels started going up along these beaches.

The resort town would only continue to grow, Sal knew, but there would come a time when it would be too crowded with tourists for his taste. By that time, though, he'd be back in the States, back in Cleveland, back in business. That fucking Ness was already out from under the protective wing of his patron, Mayor Burton; now that Burton was in the U.S. Senate, an acting mayor—Edward Blythin—was filling the slot till the next election. If the democrats won, and they probably would, that meant the end of Ness as safety director—and the beginning of Sal Lombardi finding his way home and back to the top.

Not that he was anxious. If his late cousin Angelo, God rest his soul, had thought that the life down here would make you any less a man, Sal had only to look at his wall of mounted fish and his scrapbook of hunting and fishing photos and for that matter slap his flat firm belly to know how very much a man he was. And people here, whether tourists or locals, knew Sal Lombardi was somebody important from the States. So he had respect, too. Which was important to him.

He would go back home, eventually. He even looked forward to it—but he didn't dwell on it. He was having too good a time drinking tropical drinks out of hollowed-out pineapples and watching sailboats against blue skies and divers cutting into clear water and pretty girls in skimpy bathing suits frolicking and beautiful sunsets painting the horizon.

He had learned something important here: *Salud y pesetas, y tiempo para gastarlas*—health and money, and the time to enjoy them. No accident that "tiempo" came third. Back in the U.S.A., Sal was like everybody else: a slave to watches, to clocks, marking his life in minutes and hours. These Mexicans knew enough to measure their lives in days or even years.

Time was something you let pass; you enjoyed. Something you disposed of, not let rule you. Sal was a better, happier man, now that he had absorbed this view of life. Look how Little Angelo ended up, because he was impatient; because he couldn't accept things like they were. Sal had no intention ending up that way. He was a new man. A man with a future. A man without an ulcer.

The soccer game between the good-looking young people had broken up. Sal padded out onto the white beach, his feet in sandals, a big towel rolled up under his arm. He threw the towel out and spread himself on it, belly-down; let the warmth of the sun blanket him. Bake him. Turn him blacker.

He thought about Ness, smiling into the towel as he contemplated that smug bastard being out of work soon. That fucker wasn't so much. Big-shot Ness never figured out who the Mayfield Road gang's inside man with the cops was. . . .

Vice cop Moeller—who had tipped Lombardi and Scalise and certain key others, who had lied about getting a tip from that nigger Hollis about that Democratic Party raid which was such an embarrassing fuck-up—was even now the primary police "fixer" on the east side. Even now, Moeller was serving the independent colored policy operators and Councilman Raney and the other big nigs. Even now, Moeller remained a trusted Ness associate. What a laugh. What a great big goddamn laugh!

Sal chuckled to himself as he turned over on his back, but suddenly a cool shadow fell across him. Had the sun gone under a cloud? He opened his eyes.

The silhouette of a man hovering over him blotted out the sun. Sal sat up, and the man came into focus: a big looselimbed colored man in a baggy brown suit and a misshapen charcoal fedora.

"What you laughin' about, chump?"

"Johnson?" Sal got on his feet, acting angry but in reality startled. "Jesus, Toussaint Johnson . . . what the hell are *you* doin' here?"

Johnson smiled; it was a tight smile, like a razor had cut a place in the black face for white to shine through. "You're bein' extradited, Sal," he said, pleasantly. "Vacation's over . . ."

Sal, feeling naked in his swimming trunks, gestured with open palms. "Take it easy, take it easy—there's no rush. Can't we work something out?"

"Nope."

Now Sal's anger was real. "Hey—I like it down here. I'm not ready to go back to Cleveland—not till your boss is out of office, anyway."

"Oh, you're only goin' back to Cleveland for trial, Sal. After that, you'll be headin' to prison—and then overseas."

"Overseas?"

The smile broadened. "Federal judge ordered your citizenship revoked, last week. Something my 'boss' has been workin' on for a long while. You're goin' back to Italy—after you get outa stir in five or ten years."

Suddenly Sal's stomach began to churn. To burn.

"Let's get you some clothes," Johnson said, and took Sal by the arm. "Can't get on a plane dressed like a jaybird."

Sal, almost sputtering, said, "You can be a very rich man, Detective Johnson. Name your price."

"Don't got one."

Sal laughed harshly, but it caught in his throat as he felt himself being dragged toward the hotel by the unrelenting Negro.

"You don't, huh?" Sal said. "How's one hundred grand strike you? That's a lot of money for a colored boy."

Johnson's big head was shaking side to side. "You ain't buyin' yourself outa this one, Sal. You doin' the time."

Salud y pesetas, y tiempo para gastarlas. . . .

"Then," Johnson continued, "you takes a little trip back to spaghetti land."

Sal stood his ground, jerking Johnson to a stop, breaking his grasp. "Who the hell do you think you are, boy? Eliot fuckin' boy scout Ness? Get off your high horse, Toussaint! You're no goddamn saint—you were on Rufus Murphy's payroll for years!"

"Yeah I was," Johnson said, menacingly. " 'Fore you had him killed."

Sal swallowed and looked into the black, hateful carved mask of a face, and said nothing. Sal had just learned his final Mexican lesson about time: It had run out for him, and caught up with him.

Toussaint Johnson latched onto the trembling man's arm and hauled Black Sal Lombardi, his skin burned damn near as dark as Johnson's own, off the beach and into custody.

A TIP OF THE FEDORA

As was the case with the three previous Eliot Ness novels, *The Dark City* (1987), *Butcher's Dozen* (1988), and *Bullet Proof* (1989), I could not have written this book without the support and advice of my friend and research associate George Hagenauer. George and I, individually and together, have made numerous research trips to Cleveland, visiting many of the sites of the action in this novel. We have, on these trips, haunted the Western Reserve Historical Society, where the Ness papers are kept. We both are grateful to the helpful personnel at the Historical Society, City Hall municipal reference library and Cleveland Public Library.

Despite its extensive basis in history, this is a work of fiction, and some liberties have been taken with the facts; the remarkably eventful life of Eliot Ness defies the necessarily tidy shape of a novel, and for that reason I have again compressed time, occasionally re-ordered events, and used composite characters.

Sam Wild represents the many reporter friends Ness had, including Clayton Fritchey of the *Press*, who, like the fictional Wild, was assigned to cover Ness full-time, and Ralph Kelly of the *Plain-Dealer*, who also covered the City Hall beat. Albert Curry represents the various hand-picked investigators who worked out of Ness's office, independent of the police department.

Among the historical figures included here under their real names are Mayor Harold Burton; Chief George Matowitz; Executive Assistant Safety Director Robert Chamberlin; Prosecutor Frank T. Cullitan; Albert "Chuck" Polizzi; Webb Seeley; Clayton Fritchey; Maxie Diamond; and various incidental characters, including police officers and judges.

Will Garner, the former "untouchable," is based upon Bill Gardner, who was indeed on Ness's Chicago Capone squad. To my knowledge, Gardner did not work with Ness in Cleveland; but according to several sources, including Oscar Fraley's *Four Against the Mob,* at least one former "untouchable" was on the safety director's staff of investigators. Ness did not publicize the names of his investigators, though Fraley implies in his slightly fictionalized book (most names are changed, for instance, and some dates) that this staff member was Paul Robsky. But in Robsky's own self-aggrandizing autobiography (co-written with Fraley), *The Last of the Untouchables* (1961), a work that outrageously all but omits Eliot Ness from the story of that famed squad, Robsky makes no mention of having worked in Cleveland. I chose to use Gardner as the basis for the ex-"untouchable" on the Cleveland staff because, frankly, I found him interesting.

Among the fictional characters in this book who have real-life counterparts are Salvatore Lombardi; Angelo Scalise; Toussaint Johnson; Rufus Murphy; Councilman Eustice N. Raney; Sergeant Frank Moeller; Reverend James A. Hollis; Willie "the Emperor" Rushing; Frank Hogey; John C. Washington and his wife; Clifford Willis; Sergeant Martin Merlo; Evelyn MacMillan; the Keenan brothers; and various incidental characters.

The appearance of Chester Himes as a secondary character (Katzi) in this novel is my way of giving a special tip of the fedora to this great American crime-fiction writer. The first volume of the Himes autobiography, *The Quality of Hurt* (1972), was particularly helpful in the writing of this novel.

When I was in the Writers Workshop at the University of Iowa back in the early seventies, a radical black writer was, for a time, my instructor; on the first day of class, he asked his students (all of whom were white) to name their favorite black writers. This struck me then, and now, as specious; and while my classmates dutifully mentioned Richard Wright, James Baldwin, and other predictable choices, I mentioned Willard Motley and Chester Himes. The instructor derisively dismissed Motley—because Motley's famous, powerful novel *Knock on Any Door,* detailing a slum kid's journey to the electric chair, did not focus on the "black experience."

The instructor was more charitable about Himes, though he ridiculed the author's "jive" depiction of Harlem, which (said the instructor) had nothing to do with the real Harlem. The geography, among much else, was all wrong. Over the years I've heard this criticism echoed, and it wasn't until I began writing this book—and reread much of Himes, understanding that he had spent his young (criminal) life in Cleveland, and had lived only briefly in Harlem, and spent most of his adult life in Europe—that I realized the Harlem of Chester Himes was really Cleveland's infamous Roaring Third, aka the Bucket of Blood, Bloody Scovill, and Central-Scovill.

Many of the criminals in Himes's Grave Digger Jones/ Coffin Ed Johnson stories bear the names of real black criminals of 1930s Cleveland. The real cop that Toussaint Johnson is based upon was named John Jones—a common enough name, but it's interesting nonetheless that one of the handful of black cops in Cleveland during Himes's years there shares a last name with one of his famous pair of tough fictional detectives.

In addition to Himes, numerous books on modern black history proved helpful, in particular Kenneth L. Kusmer's *A Ghetto Takes Shape: Black Cleveland, 1870–1930.* A remarkable book of photographs published by the Western Reserve Historical Society enabled me to "see" black Cleveland of the thirties: *"Somebody, Somewhere, Wants Your Photograph": A Selection from the Work of Allen E. Cole (1893–1970), Photographer of Cleveland's Black Community* (1980). Several books not specifically about Cleveland were also helpful: *Black Metropolis,*

St. Clair Drake and Horace R. Clayton (1945); *Harlem: Negro Metropolis,* Claude McKay (1940); *There Is a River* (1981), Vincent Harding; *The Autobiography of Malcolm X* (1964), as told to Alex Haley; and *Drylongso: A Self-Portrait of Black America,* John Langston Gwaltney (1980). Also, my thanks to Mary Kent Blandin, who shared with George Hagenauer her early reminiscences of the numbers game.

A much appreciated source of information on countless Cleveland subjects is the massive volume *The Encyclopedia of Cleveland History,* compiled by David D. Van Tassel and John J. Grabowski (1987), a project of Case Western Reserve University. How I wish I had had this wonderful research tool when I was writing the previous three Eliot Ness novels.

The major research source for this book, however, was the files of various Cleveland newspapers of the day, including (especially) the black newspaper the *Call and Post,* which covered many key events ignored by the white Cleveland press. A number of books and magazine articles have been consulted as well.

"A Mafia Family Legacy," a December 1985 *Cleveland Magazine* article by Stephen Sawicki, provided helpful background about the Mayfield Road gang, as did its companion piece, "The Lonardo Papers" by Edward P. Whelan.

Four Against the Mob (1961), by Oscar Fraley, the co-author with Ness himself of *The Untouchables* (1957), despite its minor fictionalizing and constant name changes, remains a helpful basic source.

A number of excellent articles about Ness have been written by Cleveland journalists. Undoubtedly the best, and probably the single most helpful source to me, is the article by Peter Jeddick, collected in his *Cleveland: Where the East Coast Meets the Midwest* (1980). Also excellent is the article "The Last American Hero," by George E. Condon, published in *Cleveland Magazine* (August 1987); Condon's book *Cleveland: The Best Kept Secret* includes a fine chapter on Ness as well, "Cleveland's Untouchable." Also helpful is the unpublished article written in 1983 for the Cleveland Police Historical

Society, "Eliot Ness: A Man of a Different Era," by Anthony J. Coyne and Nancy L. Huppert. So is an article by FBI agent George W. Arruda, "Eliot Ness–Revisited," published in the May 1988 *Investigator*. And extremely valuable is the unpublished, twenty-two-page article written by Ness on his Capone days, prepared as background material for co-author/ghost writer Fraley on *The Untouchables*.

Librarian Rebecca McFarland of the Rocky River Public Library, Rocky River, Ohio, was kind enough to send me a copy of the text of her well-researched and useful presentation, "Eliot Ness: The Cleveland Years," for which I thank her.

Other books referred to include *Mexico: An Extraordinary Guide* (1971), Loraine Carlson; *All the Best in Mexico* (1944), Sydney Clark; *Yesterday's Cleveland* (1976), George E. Condon; *Scientific Investigation and Physical Evidence* (1959), Leland V. Jones; *Crime in America* (1951), Estes Kefauver; *Mexico* (1973), Jack McDowell; *The Silent Syndicate* (1967), Hank Messick; *Cleveland–Confused City on a Seesaw* (1976), Philip W. Porter; *The Mafia Encyclopedia* (1987), Carl Sifakis; *Promises of Power* (1973), Carl B. Stokes; *Organized Crime in America* (1962), Gus Tyler.

I would like to thank my father, Max A. Collins, Sr., for sharing with me his reminiscences of his experiences as a white officer with a black crew in the Navy during World War II.

I would also like to thank my friend Tom Horvitz, who has on numerous occasions shared with me his expertise about his native city, for this as well as the previous Eliot Ness novels. Tom also lent me his last name for the composite character, Mo Horvitz, who has figured in all four Ness novels to date, in varying degrees.

Finally, I would like to thank my agent Dominick Abel; and, of course, my wife Barbara Collins, whose love, help, and support make the work possible.